**W9-AXR-087**

**"As a sworn officer of the law, I will give up my life to keep you safe. That's the truth whether you trust me to do it or not."**

She nodded, and he turned back to the coach door to listen. All he heard was her charming sigh and then her decidedly sociable voice.

"Mr. Louden?"

"Yes?"

"Is this what a cessation of hostilities feels like?"

The train whistled and started forward.

Frank looked over his shoulder. Her eyes, which had been so accusatory and antagonistic before, were softer. Kind. His feet itched to move back to the seat, to continue their conversation about him, about her, about the art exhibit this morning, if she wanted. But he held his ground because he was a marshal and she was his witness to protect.

"It's either a truce," he said, offering her his most disarming smile, "or we've both passed out from starvation."

Her lips twitched, he hoped, in amusement. "I choose your protection," she said softly.

"You don't have a choice."

**Books by Gina Welborn**

Love Inspired Heartsong Presents

*The Heiress's Courtship*
*The Marshal's Pursuit*

## GINA WELBORN

RWA-Faith, Hope & Love chapter president Gina Welborn worked in news radio writing copy until she had a stunning epiphany—the news of the day is rather depressing! Thus, she took up writing romances, because she loves happily ever afters. She is an active member of ACFW and RWA and the author of three inspirational romance novellas. A moderately obsessive fan of *Battlestar Galactica, Community* and *Once Upon a Time,* Gina resides in a wee little town outside a larger (but not large) town in SW Oklahoma. Thanks to her pastor husband's ability to spray a fabulous chemical called Demon, her children don't get to enjoy raising hunter spiders, grasshoppers and crickets. While they are (mostly) saddened, Gina is delighted.

# GINA WELBORN

# *The Marshal's Pursuit*

HEARTSONG
PRESENTS

If you purchased this book without a cover you should be aware
that this book is stolen property. It was reported as "unsold and
destroyed" to the publisher, and neither the author nor the
publisher has received any payment for this "stripped book."

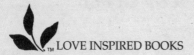 LOVE INSPIRED BOOKS

Recycling programs
for this product may
not exist in your area.

ISBN-13: 978-0-373-48724-0

THE MARSHAL'S PURSUIT

Copyright © 2014 by Gina Welborn

All rights reserved. Except for use in any review, the reproduction
or utilization of this work in whole or in part in any form by any
electronic, mechanical or other means, now known or hereinafter
invented, including xerography, photocopying and recording, or in
any information storage or retrieval system, is forbidden without
the written permission of the editorial office, Love Inspired Books,
233 Broadway, New York, NY 10279 U.S.A.

This is a work of fiction. Names, characters, places and incidents are
either the product of the author's imagination or are used fictitiously, and
any resemblance to actual persons, living or dead, business establishments,
events or locales is entirely coincidental.

This edition published by arrangement with Love Inspired Books.

® and TM are trademarks of Love Inspired Books, used under license.
Trademarks indicated with ® are registered in the United States Patent
and Trademark Office, the Canadian Intellectual Property Office and in
other countries.

www.Harlequin.com

**Printed in U.S.A.**

Do not take away my soul along with sinners, my life with those who are bloodthirsty, in whose hands are wicked schemes, whose right hands are full of bribes. I lead a blameless life; deliver me and be merciful to me.
—*Psalms* 26:9–11

To Kara-"That's some bad hat, Harry"
and Smallville-Wendy:

Ralph Waldo Emerson once said,
"It is one of the blessings of old friends
that you can afford to be stupid with them."
I say, "I'm innocent. She did it." This one is for you two.

# Chapter 1

Certainly what one is, is of far greater importance than what one appears to be.

—Emily Price Post, *Etiquette*

*Thirty-Third Street and Park Avenue*
*Manhattan Island*
*Tuesday, April 9, 1901*

She'd found the man she wanted, but if she wasn't careful—

"I will not lose this one. Not this time," Malia Vaccarelli said to no one but herself. She leveled her chin, keeping her gaze high despite the giddy tumble in her stomach as if she were a schoolgirl and not a mature woman of twenty-five. *Look confident. Be confident.*

With her beaded pochette in one white-gloved hand, she used the other to raise the hem of her white lace gown as she wove between people milling about the bricked path.

No more looking down in subordination to those more esteemed than her. No more trusting people not to steal. This time she would restrain her exuberance over "the find." This time she would be clever and sly to outwit the deep pocketbooks of her competitors.

This time she would take first prize.

Malia stopped at the steps leading up to the veranda surrounding the interior courtyard. She squared her shoulders then faced the bustling courtyard to regard Pieter Joossens, her chosen artist, at the opposite corner. The immigrant from Flanders was two decades older than any other artist at the exhibit. He spoke little English, smelled of *rookworst* and sketched in the unpopular medium of charcoals; thus, to her delight, most of her fellow patrons avoided him in lieu of the painters and sculptors. While graphite boasted a greater attention to detail, charcoal provided an unmatchable depth that Malia loved to see, loved to feel under her fingers. With the right patron— with her as his sponsor—Pieter Joossens could become the next Paul Gauguin.

*"Hij is mijn,"* muttered Malia in Dutch, a language as comfortable on her tongue as Italian and English.

Never had she been more appreciative of her ability to converse in the language of her mother's New Amsterdam ancestors. Papà and Nonno had insisted that Malia and her brother be named after Vaccarelli ancestors instead of De-Witts, so Mamma insisted on teaching her children Dutch. In secret, of course, because one did not defy Papà openly. Because of her mother's rebellious spirit, Pieter Joossens would be Malia's greatest find.

To relieve the tension twisting her insides, she breathed in the clean air shielded by the Park Avenue Hotel's seven-story walls. The string quartet's music resonated off the iron and white brick facade. Divine sounds on an equally divine spring morning. Her day could not improve.

"Miss Vaccarelli?"

She looked to the left, but the wide brim of her feathered hat shielded all but the speaker's navy trousers and polished shoes. The waiter descended to the stairs' bottom riser. As had every other hotel employee she'd encountered this morning, he knew who she was. The staff had probably been given a binder with names, photographs and a biographical summary of the Best Society attendees.

He motioned to his sterling tray, and she claimed a juice-filled champagne flute from him.

"Thank you."

His gaze lowered respectfully and he continued on.

Malia sipped her juice and glanced about. Amid the blooming and fragrant flora in the courtyard garden and on the surrounding veranda, twenty artists displayed their work in an attempt to hook one of Manhattan's millionaires who had been invited to the private showing by the Metropolitan Museum of Art. At 9:00 a.m., a little more than thirty minutes from now, the room would be opened to the public. By then, at least one artist's world would be turned upside down. A life would be changed because a socialite with more money than what she—or he—knew what to do with gave it away in the name of supporting the arts.

Until then, Malia would watch her chosen artist to ensure no one else pounced.

She continued to sip the orange juice as if she had not a care in the world, as if she were waiting on someone to join her. She wasn't—waiting for a friend, that is. As the only granddaughter of land and coal baron Gulian DeWitt, and niece to the Countess of Balwick, she knew the names of her fellow patrons and collectors, socialized with them, attended the finest schools with their daughters. Yet because of her paternal heritage, none had ever invited her into their brownstone mansions for tea, or holidays at their summer homes on Staten Island.

All that would change if her sponsorship of Pieter Joossens catapulted him to fame.

She swallowed the juice, which was sweet yet tart—just like her circumstances. Though welcomed at exclusive art shows such as this one, she wasn't "blue" enough to be accepted or welcomed in High Society. She could always marry into it. Marry up to get "in," as her defiant mother had married down to get out, or so Grandfather DeWitt regularly accused.

*No, Da, I married for love, as Malia will do.*

She smiled. How stubborn, hopeful yet romantic her mother had been.

"Ah, Miss Vaccarelli, you must tell me what amuses you."

Malia turned and managed to retain her smile despite the sourness on her tongue. Mr. Edwin Daly, Esq., was standing close. His ungloved fingers cradled her elbow as if he were her suitor, not her chief competitor responsible for wooing away the last three artists she'd offered to sponsor. Not that she faulted the artists for choosing him. A third-generation, Fifth Avenue Daly made a more prestigious patron.

"Good morning, Mr. Daly. Late, are we?" She prayed he hadn't seen her give her calling card to Pieter Joossens.

"Late?" Mr. Daly smiled, showing off his perfectly aligned teeth. He even tilted his chin to the sun-brightened blue sky so they sparkled. "Ah, my darling Miss Vaccarelli, I had to attend to business before pleasure." His fingers gave a supercilious twirl to the edge of his neatly trimmed mustache. What he intended to come across as flirtatious always struck her as slimy, an impression compounded by the way he grew the left side of his hair long and plastered it over his shiny dome.

Hopefully today the assistant district attorney would mind his manners and keep his hands to himself.

Malia handed him her empty flute. "Would you mind retrieving me another?"

His fingers curled about the glass, yet he didn't make a move to replace her drink. His dark eyes settled on hers, his breath warm and liquor-tinged. "Let's take a cruise to Newport. This weekend."

Malia raised her brows as though considering a proposal from a man whose woodsy cologne smelled out of place. The closest he'd ever come to a forest had to be pine floorboards under his feet. "For what reason should we go to Newport, may I ask?"

"So we may have time to get to know each other better."

"Would this cruise be aboard your yacht?"

"A cruiser is the perfect place for intimate conversation."

"I doubt conversation is what interests you."

He laughed. "Touché, my dear Malia. Your lack of pretense enchants me." His smile died, his tone growing serious. "What if I got down on my knee and proposed marriage? Here? Now?"

His question—uttered a handful of times over the past year—stirred nothing in her heart. Rumor had it he was courting a Newport heiress.

Malia sighed. "Please don't. You know what I would answer."

"Give me a chance to prove my feelings are sincere." He raised her hand to his lips. Despite the dozens of people in the courtyard who could notice them, and with impertinence natural to him, he brushed a kiss across her knuckles. "Someday we *will* take the first of many intimate cruises."

Malia's face warmed. Before she could counter, he dropped her hand and hurried up the stairs toward the brunch tables still brimming with fruit and pastries. She looked about the courtyard. Those who had been watching them turned back to their private conversations. Every artist spoke to someone—except Pieter Joossens. Her chosen one stood quietly and looked to be listening to an unfamiliar man in an ebony pin-striped suit as finely crafted as the one Mr. Daly wore. The handsome stranger had to be speaking Dutch because Mr. Joossens understood little English.

Malia worried her bottom lip, nerves tightening her insides. She should intervene, or at least move closer to hear what the man was saying over the other conversations and music in the bustling courtyard. *Yes, go now.*

Before she could move, J. P. Morgan's daughter, Anne, walked to the stranger and greeted him with an exuberant smile. Whoever he was, he and Anne were more than casual acquaintances. They spoke a bit. Laughed. Nodded while smiling. Anne abruptly raised a hand and motioned to her left, causing the man's gaze to shift to—

Malia froze.

He stared. At her. As if they were the only two people in the courtyard.

The right corner of his mouth eased up, and Malia couldn't breathe. Her heart beat erratically. She'd seen better-looking men, not to say he wasn't quite appealing on his own merit. His blond brows were darker than his unoiled wheat-colored hair; his jaw, sharply angled, made his face almost heart-shaped. His light blue eyes were inquisitive—no, more than that. Probing. Studious. As if he was memorizing what he saw. Even the sounds around them silenced.

Her toes itched to walk forward, to walk to him.

Then he looked past her, smiled and tipped his head.

Malia glanced over her shoulder.

George and Edith Gould descended the staircase, waving, not acknowledging her presence at all. It wasn't a direct cut, though. Like most of those in Society, the Goulds were indifferent to everything—and everyone—outside their personal concern. Miss Malia Vaccarelli wasn't significant enough to be noticed.

The stranger noticed her. *He* saw her, didn't he? She certainly hadn't imagined the connection.

She sought his gaze again, but his attention was on the talkative Anne Morgan as they walked without a backward glance—he with a slight limp to his left leg—toward a watercolor artist. Malia gave her head a little shake. How silly to think he had any interest in her. To think, even for the briefest moment, she wasn't alone amid a crowd. She would always be on the outside looking in, as one did at the glorious department store window displays, wishing she was as perfect and desirable as the products behind the glass.

Malia raised her chin, straightened her shoulders. No. She wasn't going to be that girl anymore. She was going to be confident and acquire a good standing of her own.

"Miss Vaccarelli?"

She turned to the grave voice and face of the hotel's concierge. "Yes?"

"Mr. Giovanni Vaccarelli phoned and asked that a message be delivered to you." With a we-guard-your-privacy look, he handed her a folded sheet of paper. "I secured a hansom cab. It's waiting at the main entrance." He bowed ever so slightly and walked off before she could respond.

Malia pinched her lips tight to contain her frustration. A cab waiting? In other words, she was expected to leave immediately. If Giovanni had come home last night, she would have reminded him how busy she was this morning. Not that her schedule ever mattered to him. When her brother wanted something, no one—not even family—argued. He expected everyone to be at his beck and call. No wonder he had yet to find a wife.

With a shake of her head, she tucked her clutch under her arm. She unfolded the paper, her gaze searching each end of the courtyard and veranda for the handsome stranger. He wasn't anywhere to be found.

Malia turned her focus to the sheet of ivory hotel stationery. She blinked. Her mouth fell open, the words blurring except two…*In jail.*

Giovanni arrested?

Her pulse began to race. Nonno had warned for years that the Metropolitans couldn't be trusted. Her brother was an upstanding member of the community, unlike the police, who were known for their corruption. Malia folded the paper and stuffed it back into the envelope. She hurried up the staircase, heart pounding against her chest as she wove through the crowd on the veranda. She needed to contact the family lawyers. She had to cancel her lunch meeting with Irene at Delmonico's. She had to hurry, had to—

Hands gripped her arms, stopping her on the lobby threshold. "What's wrong?"

She looked into the face of Mr. Daly and blinked repeatedly as her eyes adjusted from the brightness of the morning sky to the electric lights dimly lighting the lobby. What had he asked? What was wrong? Nothing. Everything.

"I…uh, I have to go."

"Darling, you're as white as your dress," he said with such concern that she actually believed his endearment. "I'm going with you."

To the police department? What little opening she had in Society would be closed should it become known her brother had been arrested. She gave a dismissive wave of her hand. "It's a minor family matter."

"I insist—"

"No, I—" She bit back her words and managed a serene smile. "Thank you, but I must attend to this on my own. Enjoy the art exhibit."

Malia broke free from his hold and, although the potted ferns and Grecian columns closed in around her, walked at a steady pace across the carpeted floor toward the lobby's glass front entrance. Out. *Out.* She had to get out of the hotel and away from everyone. Giovanni—the only family she had left who truly loved her, who actually spoke to her—was in trouble. She had to do whatever was necessary to save her brother.

She couldn't lose him, too.

Deputy U.S. Marshal Frank Grahame Louden followed the gaze of the angry-looking assistant D.A. to the dark-eyed beauty, one gloved hand lifting the front of her lace gown as she strolled across the lobby. The corner of Frank's mouth eased upward as he admired the enticing sway of her curvy hips. Once he finished with this pursuit, he might take a little time off to—

"Did you get her name?" Winslow asked with more than professional interest. "I think one of us should follow her."

Of course he'd learned her name, and as much as he could before Anne was distracted by a sculptor.

Frank met Winslow's questioning gaze. "Miss Morgan says the girl is a kindhearted soul who fancies art. And, judging by her coolness with Daly, she's not one of his many mistresses. She's insignificant. Besides, I heard she's not fond of men with last names that start with *W*." He patted Winslow's shoulder. "There's always Norma. She thinks you're cute."

Winslow looked dubious. "Norma said that?"

Frank's lip curled. "There's not a female in Manhattan who doesn't think that."

Winslow's grin couldn't get smugger.

"Where did Daly go?" Frank refocused on the job.

"He spoke to three men, none suspects, at the refreshment table" —Winslow withdrew a notepad from his inner coat pocket and flipped it open— "before the concierge gave him a message. He then made a call using the public phones. I caught all the numbers except the last."

"We can check them against the numbers in his file." Frank leaned against the marble column to take weight off his wounded left foot, the potted fern next to it shielding them both from Daly's view. "Anything else?"

Winslow replaced the notebook. "The meeting with O'Flaherty is off." He paused. His blue eyes met Frank's and he grinned. "Van Kelly is in custody."

Shock at the news punched the air from Frank's lungs. Now *that* was the catch of the decade. He'd have given anything to be the one to make the arrest. It would have pushed him to the top of the list as Henkel's replacement next month. His determination to arrest Billy O'Flaherty and Edwin Daly doubled. He needed to catch the pair together in the same room.

"Who caught Van Kelly?"

Winslow gave a "don't know" shrug.

Frank hoped it wasn't Ben Loskowitz, his greatest competition for the promotion.

Though New York boasted too many mobsters to keep straight, every U.S. marshal knew about Van "the Shadow" Kelly. The mafiosi boss never left a paper trail and never talked on phones out of fear of being recorded. The Secret Service had been on Kelly's tail for months in connection with counterfeiting, but the man excelled at keeping in the shadows. The file the Southern District had on Kelly contained half a page of information, amounting to almost nothing. Not even a description of what the man looked like.

"Any charges against Kelly?" He noted the hope underlining his tone.

"It sounded like none, but Daly looked worried." Winslow checked his pocket watch. "I think I'll head back to the courthouse and make a few calls."

"About the girl?" A pointless question, yet Frank hadn't been able to stop it from sliding off his tongue. His pretty-boy partner had never made it through a day of work without stopping to flirt with a lady.

Winslow adjusted his hat. "I'd be lying if I said no. She's a looker. So…you want to give me her name?"

"Not really."

While Winslow chuckled, Frank eased around the column. The mafiosi informant they'd been trailing all morning was halfway to the front entrance. "Let's see where Daly's headed. He can't be taking Kelly's arrest well."

Winslow fell into step with Frank. "I say anyone connected to Kelly should be nervous."

# *Chapter 2*

A first rule for behavior in society is: "Try to do and say those things only which will be agreeable to others."

—Emily Price Post, *Etiquette*

*Central Department of the Metropolitan Police*
*300 Mulberry Street*
*9:42 a.m.*

"**I** did not kill Mad Dog Miller." Her brother's words broke the eerie silence in the dank and stuffy meeting room. Giovanni's gravelly voiced insistence did little to abate the sinking feeling in Malia's stomach. Good thing she was sitting.

This was not a conversation one could have standing up.

"I believe you," Malia insisted. He wasn't—*couldn't*—be a murderer. Vaccarellis weren't criminals. Yet the police believed Giovanni was, which was why they'd brought him in for questioning and kept him in custody since yesterday evening, even though the witness who claimed to have seen him with Miller right before the shooting was now dead. Or so she'd been told three times already by the officer at the front desk; by Giovanni's lawyer, Mr. Sirica, as he walked her to the meeting room; and finally by her brother.

Giovanni's dark brows drew together. "You look petrified."

Tears suddenly brimmed in her eyes. "I am. For you."

"Don't be. They have no evidence."

"Two people are dead, and you're the only connection."

"I was at the wrong place, wrong time," he assured her.

"It's a frame," Mr. Sirica added.

"Malia, you can't trust a copper. Ever. They're all corrupt." Giovanni rested his arms on the table, stretching out to her. "Believe me." He sounded just like Papà and Nonno. Because of the mafiosi, Nonno had fled Sicily fifty-six years ago to create a life in America free from crime and corruption.

Malia stopped her head from shaking. "The dailies said Roosevelt cleaned up the department." She didn't know whom to believe anymore.

Under the intense gaze of the guard standing at the door and Mr. Sirica sitting at the table too, Malia gripped her brother's cuffed hands. The polished mahogany table against her bare wrists chilled her flesh, like the marble slab at Purity's Ice Cream Parlor on Broadway. Still, the room was sweltering. What she'd give for a cool breeze from the open yet barred windows to her left.

"God is in control," Giovanni whispered.

"And great is His faithfulness to us." Malia recited the words they'd often heard their parents and nonni speak, yet her faith never felt more fragile.

Giovanni's gaze shifted to the armed guard standing

beside the room's door with a hand resting on the scabbard that held his redwood nightstick. He then looked to Mr. Sirica, who immediately stopped chewing on his unlit cigar, stood and wandered over to the guard.

"Sergeant Peterson," Mr. Sirica called in a too-loud voice.

Giovanni tugged on her hands. His amber eyes met hers, steady and unashamed, as if his conscience—his soul—was as pristine and pure as her white lace dress. Giovanni leaned forward, the chest of his white-and-black bee-striped uniform against the tabletop.

"The police are waiting for the judge to grant a search warrant." He spoke in Italian and barely loud enough for her to hear. He switched midsentence to Dutch. "With your gloves on," he whispered, "open Papà's safe. 29. 5. 18. 76."

Her birthday was a combination? And why use the Italian arrangement of putting the day before the month? A pounding began between her ears, and her straw hat felt as if it bore a stuffed ostrich instead of a dove.

"Papà has no" —when he squeezed her hands, she switched to Dutch— "safe in the apartment."

"I insist," yelled Mr. Sirica, "that my client is released!"

"Sir, that's not possible," Sergeant Peterson answered.

"You have no evidence directly tying him to this crime. Or any crime. This is injustice!"

Malia glanced over her shoulder at the red-faced guard and Mr. Sirica practically nose to nose as the lawyer waved his stovepipe hat in one hand, cigar in the other, and continued to make demands the guard refused.

Giovanni tugged on her hands again, drawing her attention. "Papà's last gift to Mamma covers it."

Behind the Hackert painting?

"Take what's inside to Papà and Nonno's lawyers." The enunciation of his Dutch took on a sharp edge. His, her or maybe both their hands were sweating, yet they held firm to each other.

She nodded toward Mr. Sirica. "Why doesn't he come with me?"

"Because I need him here."

"But—"

"Papà's lawyers have a list I made, an insurance policy that will keep us both alive in the event something like this happened. They will know how to protect you until I'm released. But if the coppers find what is in the safe—" Giovanni's voice broke, and he no longer looked like a suave, polished real estate investor unjustly dressed in a horizontal-striped jail suit. No, he was that boy in the photo next to her bed—a frilly, laced-covered four-year-old holding his equally frilly, lace-covered baby sister and looking terrified that he'd drop her as their parents took their picture. "Can you do this for me, Malia?"

For family she would do anything. She nodded, although the abrupt movement added to the growing pressure in her head.

"Pray for us," he ordered. In English.

Malia stared at him. She'd given up believing his faith extended beyond Sunday attendance and dutiful giving. Even in the direst of times, he insisted she pray. True, his action annoyed her, but more so, it stoked the fear she felt for his soul.

She bowed her head and closed her eyes. Words she'd uttered every morning and night asking for her brother's protection and for his salvation fell effortlessly from her lips. Jesus was their rock and refuge. Jesus would see that the truth prevailed. Jesus desired none should perish. Her pulse steadied and the rolling in her stomach abated with each spoken praise and request. They would be all right. Everything would work out all right.

She whispered, "In Jesus's name—"

"Amen." Giovanni raised her right hand to his face, resting her knuckles against his sculpted cheek. "Even when it doesn't look like it, remember everything I am doing is to protect you. It is the duty and privilege given to me by Papà and Nonno. I will not fail. I never fail."

Malia lifted the corners of her lips, yet the smile did not reach her heart or spirit. "I love you, Giovanni. I cannot lose you too."

"Then help me. I expect you to do what you know is best." Giovanni released his grip on her hands. "Peterson," he bellowed in English, interrupting the guard's words with Mr. Sirica, "my sister is leaving."

From the chair next to hers, Malia claimed her white gloves and jade pochette that held her calling cards, lip pomade, a few coins for cab fare and the key to their Waldorf Astoria apartment suite.

Mr. Sirica rushed over and pulled her chair back as she stood.

Malia touched her brother's hand, desperate to cling. *Please, Jesus, let this be nothing more than mistaken identity.* She then turned away, leaving Giovanni in the room with his lawyer. As she buttoned on her long gloves, she retraced her path through the police headquarters' busy hallway toward the nearest stairwell. No one spoke to her, nor did she feel compelled to acknowledge anyone's presence. Giovanni spoke to her in Dutch only when he wished to share a secret. In this case, Papà's safe, and an insurance policy to keep them alive.

The latter implied someone wanted them dead.

Surely she had that wrong.

She *had* to have that wrong.

No one had any reason to want either her or Giovanni dead. Giovanni's arrest had to be a mistake. Nothing else made sense, unless this was a frame. Or…

He truly was guilty.

A death for a death—wasn't that the mafiosi way? Kill him. Kill him because he'd killed someone. But why involve her?

Pain increased under her temple. She lifted, with two shaking hands, the front of her lace skirt. As she descended the marble steps, two coppers, in long blue frocks and matching pants, climbed them. She paused midway, her shaky legs threatening to collapse, and she gripped the handrail. *Stand strong. Don't fall.* She stared absently at two rows of nine brass buttons on one Metropolitan's coat until he passed by.

The moment one inspector said "Mad Dog's murder," Malia jerked her gaze to their backs and focused on their conversation.

"Bagging Van Kelly is the coup we needed."

Van Kelly? She'd never heard of him.

"Are you going with the team once Petrocino gets the search warrant for Kelly's apartment?"

"Can't. I have paperwork to finish on Mad Dog."

"Did you hear Maranzano put a hit out on Kelly?"

"Quid pro quo for Mad Dog's murder?"

"That, and to keep him from squealing. Now we get to protect the Shadow's hide in order to give him the chair in six months. How's that for irony?"

They turned down the hallway, and their conversation faded out.

Malia opened her mouth to call after them. If Van Kelly was the one accused of the gangster's murder, and her brother was being held for the murder, then that could only mean Giovanni Vaccarelli was—

"Van Kelly?" she whispered. Her heart raced uncontrollably; her lungs struggled to grasp a breath. This couldn't be happening. Couldn't. Her brother could not be mafiosi.

"Oh dear, miss, is something wrong?"

Her legs feeling like wet pasta, Malia turned to face the older woman in a blue suit with brass buttons down the middle of the bodice. Though her face was kind, a police matron wasn't an acceptable confidante. Coppers couldn't be trusted. They had no honor. Malia had been taught that from the time she was little.

"No." Tears blurred her vision. "I need to go."

As the matron called after her, asking if she needed help, Malia hurried down the remaining steps, out of police headquarters, and onto the wide sidewalk between the buildings and street. Her stumbling walk resembled nothing learned from Miss Porter's School on how a lady was to promenade. Carriages, bicyclists, motor cars, electric cabs, hackney coaches and horse riders traversed Mulberry Street. Reporters with their cameras stood talking with patrolmen near the front stairs. Newsies held up morning papers, calling for buyers.

Malia stilled her hands from covering her ears. Never before had New York sounded so noisy. Despite the spring breeze, the air was no less dank than that inside the meeting room. She wove through pedestrian traffic and hailed a hansom cab, even though an Electrobat, with its larger front wheels than back ones, pulled up to the sidewalk first. Considering how her head was spinning, she wasn't about to ride on something that had no walls to keep her from falling out.

Another pedestrian slid onto the seat next to the driver, and the Electrobat drove off. A black hansom with a chestnut horse drew up to the curb. She reached for the side grip.

"Malia, wait!" a too-familiar voice called out.

Without a glance in Edwin Daly's direction, Malia threw herself into the cab. "The Hyphen, please," she said to the scarlet-liveried cabman through the small trapdoor in the cab's back wall. An assistant district attorney was the last person she wished to see.

*10:15 a.m.*

What business did *she* have inside the police department?

Frank leaned forward in the hansom cab parked on the other side of Mulberry Street. He flipped his marshal's star between his fingers. If he'd heard Edwin Daly yell the girl's name, there was no way he'd believe that she hadn't too, or seen Daly running to her with hat in one hand, arms flailing. Yet she had climbed into the cab and departed with haste. Warning bells clanged in Frank's ears. But warning of what? Socialite. Art patron. Rebuffer of Edwin Daly's attentions. Nothing about Malia Vaccarelli was suspicious. Except this.

Frank watched as the prosecutor looked from her retreating cab to the police department and back again as if he couldn't decide between chasing after her and going inside. The lock of hair he'd waxed over his bald scalp slipped from its mooring, shifting with each twist of his head.

Winslow crossed Mulberry Street with a group of pedestrians. He separated from the group and hurried over to Frank's cab, his cheeks flushed, his breath rushed. "Did you see the girl?"

Frank nodded and returned his attention to Daly, who still seemed indecisive as to what to do. The man was too calculating to be unsure. His action had to mean something.

"Should one of us follow her?" Winslow asked between breaths.

"I think—" Frank winced and left his sentence unfinished. He wasn't sure what he thought. Daly was their lead. The girl's appearance here could be mere coincidence, or something else. His gut told him the latter.

Daly smacked his hat against his thigh. Then he pushed

his way through the crowd toward the police department's front doors.

"Follow him," Frank ordered.

Winslow took a step away then stopped. "Are you going after the girl?"

"No." Frank pinned his badge on his left lapel. "She is connected. Somehow. The answer is in our files, and I'm going to find it, even it takes me all month."

Winslow nodded. Before Frank could say more, his partner looked to the cab driver. "Take him to Tweed Courthouse."

Malia rested against the black leather seat and breathed deep until the urge to weep passed. Had it been only an hour since she received the message from Giovanni insisting she come to police headquarters to see him? Unable to make sense of everything, she closed her eyes and prayed. Her frantic pulse slowed to a normal pace by the time the two-mile ride was over. She opened her eyes as the cab turned off Fifth Avenue. It pulled into one of the Waldorf-Astoria's ten carriage entrances on Thirty-Fourth Street, rolling to a stop on the herringbone brick path, between two Grecian columns. She withdrew coins from her clutch and handed the cabman the fare.

"Welcome back, Miss Vaccarelli," the brass-buttoned bellboy said, assisting as she alighted from the cab.

"Thank you, Henry."

"Enjoy your day!"

After a forced smile in his direction, Malia strolled across the tiled floor separating each bricked carriage lane from the other. She entered the ornate carved-mahogany-and-brass lobby that smelled of a wisteria garden and was bedazzled by the liveried bellboys, occasional dandified men in black suits, and colorful day dresses and ornate hats of the female guests. No one looked her way. There were no Metropolitans milling about the lobby, which meant the judge likely hadn't issued the search warrant yet. She still had time to do what Giovanni had asked.

With a tight grip on her clutch, she crossed the almost too-fragrant lobby to the elevators. The baroque doors opened, guests exited and she entered.

Richard, the elevator boy, smiled. "Good morning, Miss Vaccarelli."

"How do you do?" she answered.

"Very well." He adjusted his grip on the controlling rope. "Was the art show—"

"Ah, Miss Vaccarelli." Seth Prendergast, assistant to the maître d'hôtel, stepped inside the elevator moments before the doors closed. Shine from the overhead electrical light glinted off his forehead. "I've been looking for you." As the elevator began to climb, Mr. Prendergast nervously cleared his throat. "Two men were here earlier claiming they had appointments to meet with you about an art grant."

Malia frowned. She had a meeting later in the week with Miss Forrest, a painter from Boston, and tomorrow she'd arranged to meet with Pieter Joossens. Artists never initiated contact with her. "I have no appointments today."

"That's what I thought." He puffed out his chest a fraction. "Usually lounge lizards don't look so shifty, but those two wanted to know things."

"Such as?

"What time you left today. Where you go most afternoons. When you'd be back." He looked at her curiously. "I mean no offense, Miss Vaccarelli, when I say they seemed more like thugs than painters. After I spotted a gun inside one of their coats, I mentioned it to Oscar and he agreed to boot them out."

*An insurance policy that will keep us alive.*
*Maranzano put a hit out on Kelly.*

With the voices of her brother and the police echoing in her mind, Malia felt the beads of sweat on her brow. Thankfully her hat hid them from sight. If Giovanni truly was the gangster Van Kelly, would the mafiosi come after her too? She had to know what was in the safe.

Malia didn't have to look down to know her hands were shaking. "Thank you, Mr. Prendergast, for sharing this information with me." Her tone was astonishingly normal despite the panic she felt. "Please express my gratitude to Oscar for making them leave." If there was anyone at the hotel who would put her—or any Waldorf-Astoria guest's or resident's— best interests first, it was Oscar Tschirky.

The elevator stopped.

Richard opened the door. "Good day, Miss Vaccarelli."

"Good day to you both." Malia stepped out of the elevator and onto the hall carpet. She paused. Reporters were as unwelcome as lounge lizards. And once the police had the search warrant— She glanced over her shoulder at Mr. Prendergast. "Please do not let anyone know I am in the building. And, if anyone shows up asking for me, ring immediately."

If Seth Prendergast was stunned by her imperious tone, he didn't show it. Nor did Richard.

Mr. Prendergast nodded.

"Thank you," she said. "And, Mr. Prendergast, before you go, I will need a landau waiting in the carriage entrance. Give me thirty minutes." That should be enough time to unlock the safe and put the contents in a bag for transport to the family lawyers.

He nodded again.

As the elevator doors closed, Malia hurried down the hall to the suite. She unlocked the door, entered and closed it, relocking and then double-checking that the locks held. "Nettie? Are you here?"

No answer. Nettie must still be out running errands.

After dropping her key and clutch onto the mirrored mahogany sideboard, Malia dashed into the sitting room. There, above the pink velvet settee was the oil painting titled *A King Charles Spaniel in a Landscape* by Jacob Philipp Hackert. Mamma had collected hundreds of paintings, but this one of the black-and-white spaniel hung in the most prominent spot.

Malia rested her left knee on the settee and leaned forward to touch the bottom corner of the gilded frame, drawing it to the side, exposing a black Victor safe. She gasped. Some small part of her had hoped it wouldn't be here, hoped it wasn't real. But it was real. Real and staring her in the face, beckoning, taunting, mocking her for not paying attention to the suspicious things she'd seen and heard over the years.

She breathed deep and released it slowly. Again. It did little to silence the pounding in her chest. With gloved fingers, she spun the knob to 29. Her fingers trembled, yet she turned. 5. Now 18. Finally 76. Hand frozen over the handle. Pulse racing.

*Please, Jesus, let there be nothing inside.*

After another lengthy breath, she opened the door.

## Chapter 3

It is almost impossible for any of us to judge accurately of things which we have throughout a lifetime been accustomed to. A chair that was grandmother's, a painting father bought…are all so part of ourselves that we are sentiment-blind to their defects.
—Emily Price Post, *Etiquette*

Inside were a dozen butcher paper-wrapped packages, each the thickness of two books stacked one upon the other. Malia peeled back a corner. Five-dollar bills? She tore back the wrapping on two other packages—tens and fifties. A wrinkle deepened between her brows. This made no sense. Giovanni kept bills, coins and gems in a safe in his closet. As did she. No reason to have a third safe. This much money should be in a bank. Why wasn't it? She was missing something. What was she missing? Think.

She sank onto the settee, resting her head against the

wall behind her as much as her hat would allow. *Click, click* ticked the mantel clock. Ignore what she didn't know. Focus on what she did.

Fact 1: Giovanni feared the coppers finding what was in the safe, enough so that he told her about it in the one language they used strictly for passing secrets to one another. By his name and accent, Sergeant Peterson was Irish. Doubtful he could understand Dutch, but perhaps he could have known some Italian. Yet with Mr. Sirica yelling at him—

"No one could have heard or understood Giovanni's words," she said in the static loneliness of the room.

Fact 2: There was no logical reason to fear the police confiscating the money. Malia focused on the Delaroche painting on the opposite wall. What made a piece of art different enough that she would fear someone discovering? A forgery being sold as an original. She looked over her shoulder to the safe in the wall. Counterfeit? She gave her head a little shake. No. That was ridiculous. Her brother wasn't a murderer, and that money wasn't counterfeit.

Fact 3: The safe was Papà's, not Giovanni's. The suite had been their parents' after they moved out of Nonno and Nonna's brownstone seven years ago when Malia left home to attend Vassar.

Fact 4: She was supposed to take the packages to Papà and Nonno's lawyers. Her gaze settled on her hands. Giovanni had warned her to keep her gloves on. That would make sense only if one didn't want to leave any fingerprints, any evidence. She'd read Mark Twain's book *Life on the Mississippi,* in which a murderer was revealed by the use of fingerprint identification. The only people who would fear leaving prints were murderers, thieves, criminals. And gangsters. Like Mad Dog Miller, for whose death her brother was now being held for questioning, and possible indictment.

Malia stood and began to pace from one end of the living area to the other. Nonno had said the mafiosi were the reason he came to America. What if he hadn't been fleeing them? What if…he *was* them?

Van Kelly. Vaccarelli.

The facts kept pointing to guilt, to crime, to deceit by her family.

Tears spilled from her eyes. Mamma and Nonna could have known of their mafiosi involvement, or could have been as ignorant, trusting and naive as she had been. After the funeral, Grandfather DeWitt had yelled at Giovanni, saying they both knew the yacht their parents and nonni had been on hadn't sunk on accident. What if it had been a hit on them like the one now out on Giovanni? Completely possible. Plausible. And also ridiculous. Her brother did not murder Mad Dog Miller. Wrong place, wrong time, he'd said.

But she could not ignore Fact 5: Patrolmen caught him at the scene of the murder, and now the Metropolitans were banking on a search warrant to find some evidence of criminal activity. If he was innocent, he should have nothing to fear.

But if the packages of money were counterfeit…

Malia stopped pacing and looked at the printed matchbox on the edge of the settee. *Blossom Restaurant 103 Bowery Street.* Giovanni insisted he'd been down in that seedy part of town because he'd been looking at real estate development. What if he'd been delivering—or collecting—counterfeit bills? Her gaze shifted to the empty hearth. She could burn it. That meant she'd be destroying evidence, and that would make her a criminal too. How could Nonno, Papà and Giovanni sit in church every Sunday knowing what crimes they committed? Were any of their business dealings legitimate?

Her heart felt as if it were going to beat right out of her chest.

She glanced about the room, at the paintings, Italian figurines, sixteenth-century French furniture and Persian rug at her feet. Luxury built on the cornerstone of crime. *Ad vitam beneficio adficientem*—toward a life of doing good things. Not an accurate family motto.

People lied. Facts didn't.

And Fact 6 was that Giovanni told her to take what was in the safe to the family lawyers. They would know how to protect her until he was released. If the lounge lizards Seth Prendergast and Oscar had kicked out of the building were mafiosi henchmen, then what she needed most was protection. Giovanni needed some too.

Malia looked back at the printed matchbox then walked to the phone on the end table. She picked the crystal handset off the cradle. "Operator, patch me through to the law offices of Lord, Day & Lord."

*Tweed Courthouse*
*52 Chambers Street*
*That same hour*

"Could you use an extra hand?" Deputy Marshal Norma Hogan fell into step with Frank.

He paused momentarily at the entrance to the room full of desks, marshals and noise, allowing Norma to enter the room first. Three years after earning her badge, she found evidence to link two unsolved cases to a convicted moonshiner. While some marshals, lawyers and judges in the courthouse didn't like having a female marshal—and openly let her know—Frank admired grit and optimism. Norma knew how to smile in the face of adversity. Wearing a skirt didn't make her any less intimidating, when she wanted to be.

Frank stopped at his desk and nodded toward the coffee press in the back corner. "Black, with cream and two sugar cubes. I could also use lunch."

Her arched brows rose.

He pointed to his injured foot. "I'm an invalid."

She looked at him without an ounce of pity.

He laughed. "It was worth a try." He dropped the box of files and binders on the edge of his desk. "You're a woman."

"I thought you hadn't noticed."

Oh, he had noticed all right. Dimples that appeared at the barest hint of a smile. Green eyes with a slight upward tilt to the outer edges. Six feet of womanly curves she didn't hide. He'd noticed every appealing detail about Norma the first day Marshal Henkel had introduced her to his deputies, and then he filed the information away as irrelevant. His honor code meant one of them would have to quit the marshal service before he would ask her out on a date, and Frank knew full well she was as married to her job as he was. The way he saw it, Norma Hogan made a better investigator and friend than she would make a wife.

"I could use your eyes and womanly intuition." He wasn't too stubborn to admit he couldn't do this alone.

Her "Aah" had a somber edge. She pulled the chair from her desk over to his and sat. "Enough with the flattery. What plagues you?"

"Malia Vaccarelli."

"Who is she?"

Frank gave a quick rundown on the events of the morning, minus the fact he'd been unable to get Miss Vaccarelli from his mind since he made eye contact with her in the garden. He smacked the box of files. "I pulled every case that mentions Van Kelly. I need to find a connection from him to her."

She stared at him, unblinking. "You're serious."

"It's this, or put an announcement in the *Times*—Frank Grahame Louden is seeking a woman." He sat on the edge of his desk. "I do that and, next thing I know, my parents are ordering wedding invitations and I'm looking at china patterns in Gimbels."

"There may not be a connection." Norma took a file from the box. "It may have been a mere coincidence Daly showed up at the police department when she was leaving."

Frank looked longingly at the coffeepot on the other side of the room, but his aching foot demanded a rest. "Maybe, but my gut is telling me she's important. Or I think she's pretty and this is the easiest way to get her number. I need concentration juice." Leaving Norma to begin the search, he limped toward the coffee press.

"Bring me mine straight black," Norma called out over the drum of the typewriters. "Cream and sugar are for babies and love-struck marshals."

Frank stopped and looked over his shoulder. The back of Norma's head already had several ebony corkscrew strands falling from the poof she called a pompadour. "Do you think I'm going to bring you coffee like I'm your secretary?"

Norma nodded and a few more strands loosened.

"You wound me, Norma."

She chuckled. "You will bring me coffee, Louden, because no matter what else is said about you—and it's not all positive, believe me—you are a chivalrous man."

"What are you talking about? I don't have flaws."

Laughter came from too many desks around the room.

"Boys," Norma called out, "shall we let him in on them?"

Adjectives flew from their mouths quicker than machine gun fire. *Jokester. Lackadaisical. Guarded. Set in his ways. Nosy. Reticent. Unable to be serious.*

"Give a different synonym to the meaning and my 'flaws' become honorable traits," proclaimed Frank.

More laughter.

"It's true," he said, resuming his pace to the coffee press. "*Lackadaisical* is to a pessimist what *easygoing* is to an optimist, and I am an optimist."

"That's another word for *denial*," Norma quipped.

"I can be serious."

Silence.

Then someone sputtered and the laughter became contagious.

Frank rolled his eyes. He scooped coffee into the press and added hot water. He could take their ribbing. Because, before the day was over, the easygoing Frank Louden was seriously going to find what—and whom—he was looking for.

*1:16 p.m.*

"Louden, how's your toe?" Marshal Henkel of the Southern District of New York asked in that monotonously deep voice of his.

Frank glanced at the wall clock before sitting in one of the two chairs before his boss's desk. He'd worked through lunch again. "It is almost healed, sir."

"It's been a week. Are you going to tell me how you broke it?"

The overhead bamboo fan made a woodpecker-like clicking noise as it twirled.

"No, sir." Frank shifted in the wooden chair that no one in his right mind would find comfortable. He suspected that was Marshal Henkel's reason for choosing these chairs. "Is there a reason why you called me in? I'm pursuing a new lead." He and Norma had yet to find the name *Vaccarelli* in any of their files, but he wasn't losing hope.

Henkel scribbled something inside a folder on his desk, giving Frank a prime view of his gray head. "What do you know about Van Wyck Cady?"

"In his first act after taking office in January," he answered, "Governor Odell appointed Cady special prosecutor to go after members of organized crime." Frank's favorite *Times* illustrator deemed him Clean 'er Up Cady. "He is a highly respected lawyer for his rigid sense of justice. Incorruptible. Perfect man for the job."

"Ever met him?"

"Once. At a political fund-raiser my parents were hosting last year for Roosevelt."

Still looking at the folder, Henkel nodded. "Cady's first target was midlevel boss James 'Mad Dog' Miller. Miller didn't like the heat on him, so he put out a hit on the special prosecutor."

Frank found that hard to believe. "Sir, a mafiosi tenet forbids killing authorities for fear it will bring massive government retaliation."

"You expect criminals to always follow a code of ethics?"

He had a point there. "I rather hope they would," he said in a solemn tone. "It'd make our jobs easier."

Henkel glanced up. "You seem awfully serious today."

"Thank you, sir."

Henkel's lips twitched with amusement. He turned the page in the folder, occasionally underlining and writing.

Frank absently picked at a piece of lint on the black trousers of his three-piece suit as he waited for his boss to speak. Henkel's diligence and caution were well respected, especially by Frank, who prided himself on his own diligence and caution. But Frank would also be the first to admit he always struggled with impatience when waiting for Henkel to reach the point as to why he'd called a meeting.

Frank shifted as much as possible in the unyielding chair. He flexed his left ankle. The oxford he wore on that foot was a size bigger to compensate for the space his splinted toe needed, and at his desk was a padded step stool for elevating his foot. If it were possible to make the wood-planked floor in the chief marshal's office harder than that in the rest of the courthouse, he was sure Henkel had it done. The man didn't want anyone comfortable in his presence. He'd make a passable Queen Victoria.

Henkel stopped writing and abruptly met Frank's gaze. There in his eyes was an excited glint that Frank hadn't seen since the man announced he was in search of a replacement.

"Yesterday afternoon," Henkel said gleefully, "Mad Dog Miller was killed in a club on Bowery Street. In a stroke of luck, patrolmen happened to be in the area. They hauled in everyone at the scene, including a serving girl who identified the man she saw talking with Miller moments before the shooting. Another witness identified that man as Van 'the Shadow' Kelly." Henkel closed the file and rested his pen atop it. "This morning both witnesses were found dead."

Not surprising. "So Kelly was released?"

"He would have been, were it not for Malia Vaccarelli."

Frank gripped the armrests to keep from jumping to his feet. "What?"

"She is the Shadow's younger sister."

"Sister," Frank muttered. "I would have never guessed that."

"What…don't…I…know?"

Frank opened his mouth to offer a quip back, but his good sense took over. Be serious. In less time than he took to tell Norma, he updated his boss on the morning's events and finished with, "Miss Vaccarelli is the new lead

I'm pursuing." He couldn't think of a time he'd wanted to find a woman more.

"Good, good, good. Providence is favoring us today." Henkel leaned back in his chair. "An hour ago, while Metropolitans, under the watchful eye of Van Wyck Cady's associates, arrived to search Kelly's Waldorf-Astoria suite, Miss Vaccarelli and her lawyer walked into the special prosecutor's office and turned over two hundred and fifty-seven thousand dollars." He paused. "In counterfeit bills. The sourdough came from a hidden family safe."

So his girl excelled more in looks than smarts.

Frank waited until he was certain Henkel was finished. "She should have left it for the Metropolitans to confiscate.

Henkel's gray mustache twitched. "I agree."

"Why would she tamper with evidence?"

"She's a sheltered twenty-five-year-old socialite who has no clue. From what I've learned so far, she attended Miss Porter's School before earning a degree in history from Vassar. She's a volunteer at the Metropolitan Museum of Art. A mere portion of the interest from her trust fund allows her to support half a dozen artists in the New England area alone."

Frank shifted in his chair, relaxing his grip on the armrests. Edwin Daly wasn't interested in Miss Vaccarelli because of their joint love for art. He knew she was Van Kelly's sister. For someone who wanted to lengthen his tentacles in the mafiosi, a marriage to a mafiosi kin would do it. Much like Society.

"According to the girl's lawyer," continued Henkel, "Miss Vaccarelli believes the police are corrupt."

"Some are."

"Her lawyer managed to persuade her to go to Cady."

The black desk phone rang.

Henkel picked it up. "Yes?" His gaze shifted to the opened window as he listened to whoever was on the other end. "I'll have someone there in an hour." In his usual abrupt manner, he hung up the phone without a goodbye. He looked to Frank. "Cady can't charge Kelly with murder because the witnesses are dead, but he can bring him up on counterfeiting and, now that we know his real name, money laundering, which Cady wants to use to pressure Kelly into turning state's evidence. Cady isn't satisfied with one fish. He wants the whole pond."

And the pond was full of bigger fish than Van "the Shadow" Kelly.

Frank glanced again at the wall clock to the left of Henkel's desk. He needed to get back to his files. One way or another, he was going to arrest Billy O'Flaherty and the corrupt prosecutor Daly.

"Louden," Henkel said in that agonizingly slow voice of his, "your record is spotless, schooling exceptional and marksmanship perfect. I can't find a single person in the courthouse not convinced you're the best and brightest deputy I have. If you were a female, you'd be the most sought-after debutante at the ball."

And then there was that *but* coming…

"But," Henkel drawled out, "you're not living up to your potential."

Funny, his father had put it a different way: *Relying on your wit and a charming smile isn't going to get you appointed chief marshal.*

Frank leaned forward in his seat and ensured his face was devoid of all amusement. "What is it you need of me?"

"I need you to get Miss Vaccarelli out of Cady's offices without anyone noticing her and hide her somewhere safe until she can return to testify at the hearing deposition in three weeks."

Three weeks?

Frank sat very still, as a gentleman should. No wincing or fidgeting despite his annoyance. He could have Daly and O'Flaherty arrested in that time. Nannying a witness for twenty-one days sounded as enjoyable as grooming his grandmother's Pomeranian.

"Oh," Henkel continued, "and find out if she knows anything else."

"Wouldn't Norma be better suited for this job? My skills are more suited to arresting criminals than being a witness nanny."

Henkel's brows rose, yet the corner of his mouth indented slightly. "A fitting word choice. Nevertheless, because Miss Vaccarelli removed the counterfeit bills from the family safe, without her testimony, the prosecution has nothing to connect her brother to the sourdough. Van Kelly will go free, and I will do anything I can to stop that from happening." He rested his elbows on the desk, fingers steepled together, his gaze intently focused on Frank. "This is the type of high-profile job that can ensure a deputy his—or her—choice of promotions. Would you rather I offer it to Miss Hogan?"

Although Henkel had no intention of promoting Norma Hogan as the next chief marshal of the Southern District of New York, Frank understood the message. The job was his if he pulled this off. His heart, like that of a boy unwrapping his first cap gun, did a little flip. That was what he'd been working for since he joined the marshal service ten years ago.

"So, Louden, let me ask you again—how is your toe?"

"The only thing I can't do is run at full speed," he said all grim.

"Then take Miss Vaccarelli somewhere you won't have to run." Henkel offered the folder. "She's being held at Cady's office, awaiting your arrival."

"Understood." Frank stood and took the folder. "She'll be safe at my grandparents' estate in Tuxedo Park. It's gated. Police roam the grounds. My family's still on holiday in France. I'll leave a contact number with Norma."

"Good plan."

Frank stepped to the office door.

"Louden?"

Anxiety fluttering about his stomach, he looked to his boss. "Yes?"

Henkel's eyes narrowed. "Mess this up and you'll be processing evidence for the rest of your career."

Frank nodded. The warning was clear.

He started to leave then stopped. Something nagged at him. Something didn't make sense. "Sir, Van Kelly hasn't survived in the shadows on his own. He needs minions to do his dirty work, connections to protect his identity."

"Go on."

"Why not send one of his lawyers, a minion or a copper he buys off to collect the sourdough? Why would he send his sister to do something that put her directly in danger?"

Henkel leaned back in his chair, tapping his steepled fingers together. "Good question. That's something you need to figure out."

# Chapter 4

If you have, through friends in common, long heard
of a certain lady, or gentleman, and you know that
she, or he, also has heard much of you, you may say
when you are introduced to her: "I am very glad to
meet you," or "I am delighted to meet you at last!"
—Emily Price Post, *Etiquette*

*Twenty-Third Street and Fifth Avenue*
*2:08 p.m.*

"Miss Vaccarelli, you understand now that you've done
this, your life as you know it is over?"

With her hands clenched together in her lap, Malia
didn't flinch under the hazel-eyed gaze of Special Prosecutor Van Wyck Cady. She was too emotionally and
physically exhausted to feel much of anything. The gaunt
six-footer standing with his back to a wall of law books

was—as the papers described him—ramrod straight, not only because of his bearing but also because of his personality. Still, the least he could do was show a mite of compassion and gratitude, as a true gentleman would.

Moments after entering the law offices of Everts, Cady, Powell and Perkins, she'd been hidden in a back room with her lawyer and a stenographer who refused to look at them. Special Prosecutor Cady had questioned her on what she knew, why she brought the bills to him, what she wanted in exchange for her testimony. The latter had rankled. Her foremost desire was to help her brother. At the most, he'd serve eighteen months for possession of counterfeit bills, as explained by her lawyer—and closest friend—Miss Irene Gibbons, the first female barred associate at Lord, Day & Lord.

Malia hoped turning in the counterfeit bills—sourdough, as Irene called them—would motivate her brother to change his ways. She wanted Giovanni to live a God-honoring life. Her fear of losing him forever had made her desperate. Her love for him made her brave. Yet for the past hour—maybe longer—she and Irene had sat on a tan linen sofa in the law office library with nothing but the sounds and view of the construction on the triangular-shaped building across the street.

*Did* she understand, now that she'd done this, her life as she knew it was over? "Sir, I'm not sure what you mean."

"Then let me explain," Cady bit off. "No more volunteering at the Museum of Art. No more apartment suites at the Waldorf-Astoria. No more shopping on the Ladies' Mile. No more balls, operas, book clubs and charity events. No more evenings of drinking tea and playing dominoes with your brother. Everything you know is at an end."

He was being a bit dramatic.

She looked to her lawyer. "It's not going to be like he says. Why would it all have to end?"

Irene, in a chiffon-and-velvet day dress as black as Malia's lace gown was white, wrapped her hands around Malia's. "How about we take this one day at a time? I'll be with you every step of the way."

Malia nodded then looked to Mr. Cady, who clenched a leather binder and looked at her as if she was the village idiot. "Sir, my life as I knew it was over the moment I saw what was in the safe." That everything would change as he claimed, she wasn't convinced. "I haven't changed my mind about testifying at the deposition hearing, but I want protection on Giovanni increased. His death doesn't benefit either of us."

He didn't respond.

"Mr. Cady," Irene said, "that Maranzano put a hit out on Van Kelly makes me suspect Mr. Vaccarelli knows more than what his fellow gangsters want shared. The most you can get him on is possession of illegal currency, and that is only with my client's testimony. It's in your best interest to keep him alive and convince him to talk."

Mr. Cady tapped the binder against his thigh, his lips in a thin line. Malia couldn't tell if he didn't like being told something he knew, or didn't like being told it by a female who was as smart as any male lawyer *and* pretty as a Gibson Girl.

A knock resounded on the library door, which then opened. A secretary stepped inside the room. "Sir, the deputy marshal is here."

Mr. Cady nodded. "Send him in."

She stepped to the side. A blond man, as tall yet bulkier than the special prosecutor, entered. He wore a silver star on his left lapel and a scowl on the very face Malia had seen that morning at the Park Avenue Hotel. She held her breath. It was him—the handsome stranger. Only now his formerly clean-shaven face bristled with whiskers, and two guns hung on the belt at his waist.

Good gracious, he had better not be here for her.

"Frank!" Irene stood, smiling, and met the marshal next to the round mahogany table in the middle of the library where both Irene's and Malia's hats rested. "I'm glad Henkel sent you." If he was uncomfortable with Irene's exuberant handshake, he didn't show it.

"I wasn't expecting to see you."

"Same goes here. After I insisted on protection for my client—" Irene glanced at Malia. "I'm so sorry I didn't tell you about my request earlier." She turned back to the marshal. "I expected Henkel to send Winslow." Malia noted the wistfulness in her friend's tone.

"Winslow's tracking a lead," he answered matter-of-factly.

Irene introduced him. "Van Wyck Cady, Frank Grahame Louden."

The men shook hands and exchanged "How do you do?" and "Nice to meet you."

Irene then said, "Frank, this is my client, Miss Malia Vaccarelli, the one you are here to protect."

The marshal looked Malia's way. His intense blue eyes studied her for longer than made her comfortable, enough that Malia stood at the same moment he said, "You're Van Kelly's sister." He voiced it as one would say *turncoat*.

Maybe Irene was right that not all coppers were corrupt, but how was Malia to know a good one from a bad one? She looked about the room for another means of escape. Across the library was a second door, but she had no idea where it led. And if the marshal's build was true to form, she doubted she'd make it to the door before he caught her. Or maybe she could, considering how he favored his left leg.

He followed up with a smile and a cordial, "I am very glad to meet you."

She was supposed to be polite and say, *I'm delighted to*

*meet you too,* but she wasn't delighted or glad or pleased or relieved. She wanted him gone. Or her gone without him.

"Irene?" she said with a serenity that belied her nerves. No matter how fearful she felt, she would maintain good form as a lady should.

"Yes?"

Malia curved her lips a bit, just enough to imply sweetness. "I am not going anywhere. With him."

He wasn't keen on going anywhere with *her.*

Since he couldn't admit that and still be a gentleman, Frank rested a palm on the hilt of a gun. He tried to think of something—anything—to say to the beauty standing no more than four strides from him. What he'd give for her to be dowdy, or at least have an oversized Roman nose, not *this.* Her lashes were as dark and sooty as her hair, a compelling contrast to the paleness of her golden skin. Of course, the paleness likely resulted from her being anxious, which he could tell by the way her elegant fingers nervously picked at her lacy skirt. She probably had no idea she was doing it.

He cleared his throat. Twenty-one days guarding *that.* At breakfast, he'd even thanked God for no female in his life to distract him from his work. If he were a cynical man, he'd swear he heard heavenly laughter.

"Why won't you go with Frank?" Irene asked, reminding him there were others in the room besides themselves.

"That's something I'd like to know too," Cady put in.

Miss Vaccarelli snatched her fancy clutch off the linen sofa. "Coppers are corrupt."

Cady shrugged as if it was something he'd heard before.

"I'm not a copper," Frank clarified. "I'm a deputy marshal of the federal court of New York. I can be trusted."

Irene nodded.

Miss Vaccarelli looked down her perfectly pert nose

at him, as if to say lawmen were all the same to her. That is—unprincipled. Crooked. Evil.

With his middle finger, Frank tapped the side of his gun. The woman was as stubborn as she was naive and snooty. Not to say he wasn't pleased to discover her flaws. By the time they made it to Tuxedo Park, he expected to have a page-long list of inadequacies to make her more unappealing to him. He didn't want to imagine what she looked like happy and laughing. She looked ravishing enough being angry and afraid.

"Frank is here to help," Irene offered. "You can trust him as you trust me. As you trust Special Prosecutor Cady."

Cady concurred.

Miss Vaccarelli's lips pursed tighter than the button-tufted back of the sofa, drawing Frank's attention to the mole—no, beauty mark—just above her rose-colored lips, details he certainly should *not* be noticing. But now that he had, he couldn't quite find the wisdom to look away.

"I can't." She shook her head and took another step closer to the library's side door. "Irene, I don't need a marshal to guard me. Giovanni promised that Papà's lawyers will ensure my safety."

Frank's inner warning bell sounded. He and Cady exchanged glances. Cady then nodded, giving Frank leave to ask what he knew they were both wondering.

As to not frighten her more, Frank gently asked, "How could he promise that?"

She looked to Cady, her gaze direct and unshrinking. "Sir, I've answered all your questions. May I leave?"

"I, too, need to know why your brother promised that."

"Is there something you haven't told us?" Irene put in.

Miss Vaccarelli's confused gaze shifted to each person in the room. Either she was a splendid actress or the most guileless woman Frank knew. His gut told him the latter.

He knew too many unscrupulous women—coquettes who knew how to use their wiles for their benefit—to know she was an innocent, a socialite who didn't have a clue. Protect her, he could. Ensuring she didn't do something stupid on her own—now that would be the tricky part.

She nipped her bottom lip and stayed silent for some moments. "My brother made a list and gave it to the family lawyers. He said it was an insurance policy to keep us both alive in the event he was arrested."

"Why am I just hearing about a list now?" Special Prosecutor Cady demanded.

She stared at him, her eyes still devoid of any deception, her expression slack. "It didn't cross my mind. I explained after I arrived that Giovanni asked me to take the counterfeit bills to the family lawyers, and that they would protect me until he was released from police custody. I never intended on withholding pertinent information."

"But you did," groused Cady.

Her shoulders straightened, eyes narrowed as she took her leisure meeting each of their gazes. "Considering the character I demonstrated in turning over the sourdough," she said, bringing a pretty color to her cheeks, "I see no cause for any of you to decry a minor omission on my part."

Frank raised a brow. She was a feisty one.

Irene sighed. "I'm your lawyer, and my job is to protect you. You should have first told me about the list."

"Why?" Miss Vaccarelli's voice rose. Her eyes filled with tears, which only brightened the amber color. "I have no idea what's on it. Until I spoke with Giovanni this morning, I had no idea he was mafiosi, which I am still struggling to believe." Her gaze settled on Frank. "Being sheltered from my family's apparent mafiosi involvement does not make me obtuse."

"We don't think that," Irene put in.

Cady said nothing.

Nor did Frank.

Her hands tightened around her beaded clutch. "What could possibly be on this list that would stop someone from wanting to kill my brother? Or me?"

An idea came to his mind, but it wasn't his place to say. Instead of answering, the two lawyers approached each other and held a whispered conversation. Miss Vaccarelli breathed deep then dabbed her eyes with the tips of her fingers, a womanly action he'd often seen his grandmother do. On the edge of his tongue were the words to tell her that all would be well. Given time. She needed to trust the court, Irene and him to protect her.

"Well?" prompted Miss Vaccarelli.

With a deep furrowed brow, Cady motioned to the table with his binder. "I need you to look at this—"

"No, Mr. Cady." Her gaze bore into the special prosecutor's, unflinching. "I will not look at anything until someone tells me what you all know and I don't."

Cady looked at her askance, in the same manner as Frank had seen him in the courtroom with an uncooperative witness. "Miss Vaccarelli, I have the authority to place you in jail for—"

"Accomplices," Frank filled in, cutting off the prosecutor's threat.

Irene added, "Gangsters he fed the sourdough to."

Cady grabbed Miss Vaccarelli's arm, and she gasped as he dragged her to the table.

"There's no need for that," Frank ground out. "She's a lady."

"She also knows more than she's telling." Cady shoved her onto a seat and slapped the binder down in front of her. He opened to the first page. "Have you seen this man before?" He pointed to a picture.

Although it was upside down, Frank could tell it was of

Albert "Fingers" Bolz. He'd arrested the gangster twice, and twice watched the courts set him free because of lack of evidence. Edwin Daly had been the prosecutor both times.

Miss Vaccarelli rested her clutch on the table. Her eyes darted from the binder to Irene then to Frank. The square-tipped edge of her chin rose. She didn't have to speak for him to hear *I will not answer as long as he is present.*

Cady drew in a long, angry breath through his nose. "Miss Gibbons," he warned.

Irene rushed to sit in the chair next to Miss Vaccarelli. "Malia, please. It is in your best interest to cooperate."

Miss Vaccarelli, though, kept eyeing Frank, her gaze defiant, yet the hand holding her clutch had a slight tremble. Out of fear? Or anger?

He opened his mouth to offer to leave the room then thought better of it. They had to spend the next three weeks in each other's presence. The girl could start getting used to him—start getting over her misgivings about him—now. He crossed his arms over his chest.

"Malia," Irene gently prodded. "I shouldn't think you would enjoy jail."

Without the asperity of a retort, Miss Vaccarelli looked to the binder. "I've never seen him before."

Cady turned the page. "Either of them?"

Frank watched her intently. The gangster on the left was Billy O'Flaherty.

"No." Her eyebrows furrowed then relaxed. Before he could turn the page, Miss Vaccarelli placed her palm flat in the middle of the binder. "Who are these men?"

"Known gangsters," Cady answered.

"And you think I know them?" Her expression was as incredulous as her tone.

Cady pointed to the bottom of a page. "Some go by their real names. Others, like your brother, use a fake one because they have legitimate business dealings, and families they want to protect. That your brother was involved in counterfeiting means we now have just cause to investigate him for money laundering. He could go to jail for a long time."

She released a weary breath and turned the page. "No." Another page. "No." And another. She frowned, leaned forward. "That's Mr. Heilbert, Patrick Heilbert. He leases space in one of my brother's buildings for his grocery. He can't be a gangster. He is the kindest man and most devoted father you will ever meet."

"Miss Barn," he said to the stenographer, "note that Miss Vaccarelli identified Patty Nundel as Patrick Heilbert."

"Are you serious?" She stared at him, unblinking. "He'd been attending seminary to become a priest when his father died. He gave that up to take over the family business, to care for his mother and sisters."

Cady turned the page. "Keep looking."

"This is wrong, all wrong," Miss Vaccarelli muttered yet resumed her perusal.

Frank took a seat at the table. As casually as he could, he rested his wounded foot upon another chair. Miss Vaccarelli flipped another page. Minutes passed and Irene grew paler and a bit green as her client identified seven additional gangsters, five of whom the authorities hadn't had real names for, before reaching the last page in the binder.

"Malia," she whispered, touching her client's hand and stilling her from closing the binder. "Have you ever seen any of these men together?" The look in her eyes said *please say no*.

"Once," Miss Vaccarelli answered.

Frank felt a bit green himself.

Cady placed a hand on the table and the other on the back of her chair, leaning down. "When was that?"

"Three days ago," she answered matter-of-factly. "Giovanni had been ill the night before, from eating bad shellfish, so I cut short a meeting with the volunteer coordinator at the Museum of Art. Four of them, and another man I didn't recognize, were in the living room discussing how to help a needy business associate. Giovanni offered to take care of Mr. Miller, which frustrated me. I walked in and said he had no business caring for another person in his condition and that I would take care of Mr. Miller if he would give me the address. Giovanni was furious with me. The men laughed then each gave my brother their support and—"

Her eyes widened. Her hand covered her mouth, her head shaking.

"Oh my," she whispered.

An *oh my*, in Frank's opinion, didn't describe how deep the mire she was in.

The stenographer looked up from where she sat in the corner. Her pencil fell from her hand. Her jaw sagged. Irene didn't look as if she was even breathing. The man known for his gifted oratory, Special Prosecutor Cady, stood straight, a hand on his forehead.

No one had to say anything for Frank to know they were all thinking the same as he.

Malia Vaccarelli had unwittingly walked into a mafiosi meeting and heard her brother vow to kill James "Mad Dog" Miller. She could also identify four other gangsters who knew of the hit and agreed to it—a hit to take out the very man who intended to kill Special Prosecutor Van Wyck Cady. The fifth man could have been Maranzano, who, like Van Kelly, they didn't have a photograph of. If she wanted to stay alive, Malia DeWitt Vaccarelli needed more than what was probably a list of men her brother was funneling counterfeit bills to.

Frank rested his foot on the floor with more force than

he intended, causing the splint to thump against the shoe, sending a jolt of pain shooting up his leg. This day grew exponentially worse for both of them.

He leaned forward, elbows on the table. "Miss Vaccarelli." He waited until her expressive brown eyes met his blue ones. "You need my protection, whether you want it or not."

## Chapter 5

[In] fashionable society an "escort" is unheard of, and in decent society a lady doesn't go traveling around the country with a gentleman unless she is outside the pale of society.

—Emily Price Post, *Etiquette*

*3:08 p.m.*

Twenty-seven minutes. That's how long she'd been waiting. Not that anyone seemed to mind but her.

Malia paced the library's carpeted floor, circling the mahogany center table in a room that still smelled like the lemon-and-garlic remains of the lunch Irene had ordered from Delmonico's. She listened to the wall clock; waited for her lawyer, the marshal, and Special Prosecutor Cady to return; and tried to stifle her growing panic. Every door was locked. As were the windows.

She'd tried them all. Someone—everyone—didn't want her to flee.

She looked past the shelves of law books to the row of windows, the sky blue and clear and sunny. Because they were on the seventh floor, the tips of several buildings were visible nearby and in the distance. When Giovanni looked through the window in the police department, did he see what she saw? She was no freer than he was.

The clock continued to tick.

She continued to pace and pray, but mostly pace.

Twenty-nine minutes.

Thirty.

Thirty-one.

Thirty—

The door opened. "I'm so sorry it took so long," Irene said, rushing inside, her breathing harried. Miss Barn, the shy stenographer, followed close behind.

Malia stopped pacing. "You said you would be gone only a few minutes."

Miss Barn closed the library door.

"I know, I know." Irene looked as flustered as she sounded. "But Cady didn't agree with Frank on what to do with you. Once we came to an agreement, there were arrangements to be made, phone calls." She took the tan leather trench coat and straw hat from Miss Barn then walked to Malia. "Frank and Cady walked around the building's perimeter and didn't see anyone suspicious, but we can't take any risks. You need to put these on."

"I have a hat." Malia reached for her white feathered one in the middle of the table, but Irene grabbed it first.

"Sorry, you can't keep it. It fits the description of what you were wearing at the art exhibit." She gave it to Miss Barn, who kept her gaze on the ground. "Hat for a hat."

Miss Barn whispered thanks.

"If my dress would have fit you," Irene went on, "I'd

have happily exchanged because black is far less conspicuous than white. Seeing that the good Lord blessed you with more of…well, everything than He did me, I had to find someone more suitably matched. Miss Barn became the lucky volunteer." She handed Malia the coat. "Frank said a coat would do."

Malia's lips came together to ask Miss Barn if she felt lucky or volunteerish (for she looked neither), but before she could utter the first syllable, Irene demanded she put on the coat.

"Hurry, Malia," she added as she opened Malia's pochette.

Malia drew the trench coat on over her dress. Considering the minimalism of Miss Barn's white blouse and gray skirt and her lack of jewels, the coat was likely the most expensive item the stenographer owned. Malia didn't want to calculate how many months of putting money aside that the girl had to do. Inside *her* closet in her Waldorf-Astoria apartment were at least a dozen coats, capes and stoles, including a supple lambskin coat from Italy that Giovanni had bought her the same day he bought his petromobile, and a pair of slink gloves that she'd never been able to move past her revulsion to wear.

The way Miss Barn held Malia's hat—

The poor dear clung to the brim in desperation not to give it up, yet her brow furrowed as if she were trying to convince herself that this was a joke and any minute Irene would laugh and, like a bad Santa, take back the hat.

Irene, being Irene, did nothing of the sort. She withdrew the apartment key. "I'll hold this for you until you return, and I will make arrangements with Pieter Joossens like I promised." She handed Malia the clutch, which Malia took and held to her chest.

Malia shifted her weight uncomfortably. "What am

I supposed to do for three weeks with only one set of clothing?"

"Frank has that taken care of."

"What do I do if I need to contact you?"

"Frank will help you."

"But what if he *is* my problem?"

Irene clearly saw Malia's distress, and didn't look the least bit concerned. "Frank is the best there is. I'd be in love with him myself if it weren't for— Well, that's neither here nor there."

Malia didn't say a word. There was no point. Once Irene set her mind upon something, nothing—neither hell, nor high water, nor a handsome man—could change it. Malia admired that about her. Until now. Sometimes she suspected Giovanni's courtship of Irene in the six months following the funeral was so Malia and Irene could become friends. Malia and Irene had attended the opera together more than Giovanni and Irene had.

Irene gripped the sides of Malia's arms. "As your lawyer, I advise you to trust Frank."

Malia felt her upper lip curl.

"As your friend…" Irene leaned forward. Placing her cheek against Malia's, she whispered, "Look away when he smiles. Trust me." Then she was off like a rabbit to the door. "Hurry. Frank likes to stay on schedule."

Frank. Frank. Frank, Frank, Frank. Frank.

She hadn't even begun her three weeks with him and she was sick of his name.

Malia pinned the straw hat atop her head. She collected her gloves from the table and walked to Irene, Miss Barn silently following.

Irene opened the door a smidgeon, peeked and then opened it the rest of the way.

"Wait." Malia turned around, and Miss Barn stopped in front of her. "Thank you." She laid her gloves across her pochette and offered them to Miss Barn, whose pale blue eyes immediately widened.

"Oh, I cannot accept—"

"Please," Malia cut in, "allow me. Gloves and clutch for a coat? It seems only fair. We can always trade back."

Miss Barn hesitated. With her translucent skin, flaxen hair and quiet demeanor, she had blended into the room, unnoticed as the pale brows on her face.

Then she looked up and smiled.

Malia did too.

*Grand Central Depot*
*Forty-Second Street and Fourth Avenue*
*3:42 p.m.*

Nearly nine hours after she first saw him in the Park Avenue Hotel courtyard, he led her into a wall of smoke.

Eyes burning, Malia blinked as she blindly walked next to the marshal. If he weren't clenching her hand in his— and it was quite embarrassing that he was—she would have lost him in the darkness. An engineer led them through the workers' passage in the shadowy and noisy Park Avenue tunnel, filled with smoke from the hundreds of steam locomotives arriving daily. A rate of one every forty-five seconds, or so the *Times* recently reported. She'd never concerned herself with trains or the political views of boosting public safety by removing the locomotives from Manhattan's surface and putting them underground. As if digging for the subway wasn't enough. Street construction was a way of life in the city.

The last time she had been at Grand Central was when the train brought her home following her graduation from Vassar. Other than an occasional visit to the outer boroughs, she'd simply had no need—or inclination—to leave the island since. She still had no inclination.

Need, though…well, that was debatable.

Not that the marshal listened to her any more then Irene or Mr. Cady had. They'd seized control of her life and decisions as if she were a child, sending her into the unknown, with no one but a questionable stranger as her escort. For all she knew, he could be taking her to Maranzano, the gangster who'd put the hit out on her brother.

Her chest tightened, and breath fled from her lungs. She couldn't do this. She couldn't leave Giovanni. They had only each other. She had to get out of the tunnel, get away from the marshal. Home, she had to get home. She'd be safe there in the Waldorf.

"Here's your train," the engineer called out.

No time. She had to run.

The marshal drew her close, his palm warm against hers. Malia pulled to no avail. His blue eyes narrowed ever so slightly in annoyance upon guessing her intention. Had she a wild look in her eyes? Ashen complexion? Or had her frantic pulse given her away? Yet he uttered no condemnation or chastisement as, like a doting suitor, he gallantly helped her onto the platform and over the threshold of the private coach.

"My wife," the engineer was saying, "wanted to elope."

"Why didn't you?" the marshal asked.

Malia left him to continue the charade he'd created to explain their need to sneak onto the train instead of going through the depot's main entrance, where people could be looking for them. Amazing what a few crisp hundred-dollar bills would get a man. She moved past a sofa and a set of chairs, turning on the electric lamps. She paused at the dining table in the center of the coach.

They were to wait thirty minutes before the train had to move to the platform for passengers to begin filling the Shore Line Express. The plan was cleverly laid, or so Irene had stated. They would go to Boston, slip immediately onto

the night express back to New York, and then take a train
to somewhere on Long Island where they were to hide out
for the next three weeks. He'd even left the name of another marshal to contact in case of an emergency. Irene
would provide a cover for Malia's disappearance: she went
to visit her aunt and cousins in England. All Malia had to
do was what the marshal had asked before they sneaked
out the back entrance of the special prosecutor's office
building—trust him to keep her safe.

Safe? From whom?

Perhaps people wanted to harm her—Mr. Maranzano
sprang to mind—but she'd yet to feel any danger, except
that coming from the marshal. She was a socialite, an heiress, an art patron whose life was so dull and ordinary that
reading in the *Times* about a traffic block near the Brook-
lyn Bridge was the most excitement she experienced during any given week. She wasn't worth killing. She just
wasn't worth it.

Her eyes blurred.

Something between a cough and a chuckle—yet completely hysterical—burst from between her pressed lips,
breaking the stalwart composure she'd held for hours in
the name of good behavior. While the marshal and engineer continued to speak outside, she ran to the back of
the coach. The door handle rattled. Locked. Pinching her
eyes closed, she clenched her lips until the need to scream
passed.

Malia slowly drew in a breath, crossing her arms, rub-
bing her sleeves. She couldn't escape. Not from the coach.
Not from her family. Not from him. Even if she did get
free, the marshal would find her. He'd pursue her to the
last place on earth she tried to hide. Because he knew
what he was doing. Because she was naive. But mostly—
she sighed—mostly because she was weak and powerless

and afraid. Her arms fell limp to her side, the sour taste of defeat growing in her mouth.

Malia flicked on the lights in the extravagant Pullman car. Brass and crystal lamps. Rosewood-paneled walls. Gold velvet chairs with fringed trim that matched the heavy drapes.

She removed the ankle-length traveling coat and straw hat of her "disguise." Soot dusted the tan leather, which meant she had soot on her. She certainly couldn't lay the coat on one of the chair seats. She found a closet. Inside were numerous wooden hangers. Malia then stepped to the lavatory. After hanging up the coat, she opened cabinets, found a cloth and dampened it. She then washed her face and neck before pulling the pins from her chignon and shaking the soot from her hair.

She sought her exhausted reflection in the mirror. Tears welling again, she drew her waist-length hair back from her face, twisted it to form a rope then coiled it into an Apollo knot atop her head. She pinned the knot in place. Her enlarged pupils made her eyes look like a spooked owl's; her skin was the color of a corpse. Following a slow exhale, she turned to the coat and began to brush the soot off the surface.

She had to focus on something—anything—and give her hands something to do to keep her mind from replaying the day's events. The monotonous repetition of cleaning brought comfort, silence amid the solitude, soothing her erratic pulse.

She had both sleeves cleaned when the marshal's imposing presence appeared in the doorway, two feet from her, soot-dusted and looking uncharacteristically amused. Of course, his amusement could be native and the scowls she'd received uncharacteristic, but until she knew him better—and she never intended to—an oddity his amusement would be. He didn't say anything right away. Instead his gaze shifted from the coat to the damp and soiled cloth in her left hand. Her soot-tinged fingers flinched. Her heart gave a tight, panicky squeeze.

Tossed by a wave of embarrassment, she fought the urge to hide her hands behind her back. She had no reason to feel ashamed, but that look in his eyes when he'd walked into the law library—

As if her soul was tainted. Dishonorable. Unforgivable. Unclean.

*That's not me,* she wanted to scream. *You have me pegged all wrong.*

"May I be of service?" he said in a helpful tone, which she didn't buy for a second.

A woman could tell when a man had ill feelings toward her, not that she would be so rude as to tell him she knew. Her feelings for him grew in the same field. Nevertheless, they were stuck together by request of her lawyer and the insistence of the special prosecutor. She ought to be cordial. Good form dictated it.

Malia inclined her head to the soot ring around the marble sink. "Are you certain you wish to help?"

"I insist."

"Yes, you would," she murmured.

He chuckled at that.

She couldn't imagine how anyone enjoyed his company; he was an odd sort. His moods shifted like the winds from the Atlantic. Serious then jovial. Noble then inconsiderate. Yet there was one consistent thing about him—

"You always like to have your way, don't you?" she asked, gripping one of the coat's wooden buttons.

"Yes." He leaned a little closer, enough that she caught a whiff of his cedar-and-spice cologne. Although he didn't grin, he clearly looked as though he wanted to. "I suspect you do, too."

She clamped her mouth shut—most would say a wise

decision, considering the lack of polite responses milling about her mind. Giovanni was the selfish one in the family. She was the one who made the sacrifices to keep him happy. She'd always earned compliments from their parents and nonni on her ability to always be kind to others.

The train shifted forward; Malia hit the sink with her hip before grabbing the brass towel rack to steady herself. The marshal wobbled yet held his balance.

He gave her a strange look, as if he were actually concerned. "Are you all right?"

Though her hip throbbed, she nodded then stopped at the sudden dizziness. She clung to the towel rack until the spinning stopped.

"Miss Vaccarelli, when did you last eat or drink something?"

The sincere concern in his inquiry gave her pause.

*You can't trust a copper. Ever. They're all corrupt.*

Giovanni hadn't had to repeat what she had heard all her life for her to remember Nonno's warning. She'd also believed the Vaccarellis were a law-abiding family, and now the evidence pointed in the opposite direction. She didn't always have to have her way, but she hated being wrong. She didn't want to be wrong about the marshal too.

She needed a constant.

She needed him to be corrupt.

The marshal looked at her with a brazenness that reminded her of Edwin Daly. Not brazenness. Chutzpah— yes, that's what the marshal had. For all his flaws, Mr. Daly knew art, loved it more than his job. What did this man love, know and breathe? What gave the marshal personal confidence and courage? What reigned in the core of his soul to give him that assured serenity he wore like a cloak? What—?

Stop! Who he was didn't matter to her. No more pondering him. In three weeks, she would walk, to her delight, out of his life and never see him again.

Malia shook the soot off the damp cloth into the sink and resumed wiping the coat. "I ate earlier with Irene. Tuesdays are our weekly lunch date at Delmonico's. Fridays we have dinner. Instead of eating at the restaurant for lunch, she had it delivered to—" She cut herself off upon realizing her chattiness. He didn't care to know this. She was insignificant to him.

She didn't have to turn her head to know he continued to study her. The man had perfected the art of thinking before speaking.

Then he broke the silence with, "The next twenty-one days will be more pleasant if you would start trusting me."

"You're a stranger to me." Malia kept her attention on the coat. She wiped the collar. "I have no cause to trust you."

"Neither do you have cause to distrust."

"You. Are. A. Copper."

"I'm a marshal. Not all coppers are corrupt."

She turned to him. "Then tell me what you're hiding."

"Hiding?" His eyes widened, stunned. "I am not hiding anything. You, on the other hand, have already proved you will withhold information," he pointed out.

"I didn't—" With a grumble under her breath, she tossed the cloth into the sink and gave him her full attention. "What were you doing at the art exhibit this morning?"

"Following a lead."

"Me?"

"No."

"Then who was it?"

"That's not information you need to know."

Then what did he think she needed to know? Nothing? Shield her because she was a woman, therefore too fragile to handle the truth. Shield her as the Vaccarelli men had because they didn't— Her chest flinched as if it'd been pierced, which it had, figuratively, by her family, and she was realizing the depth of it only now. Her family hadn't trusted her with the truth about them.

"What you are saying," she said with deliberateness, "is that you don't trust me with information because you don't believe I can be discreet. Or loyal. Why should I extend to you what you are unwilling to extend to me?"

Frank ran a hand through his hair, soot dust sprinkling to the carpeted floor. She was a witness. What he was doing at the exhibit was classified information. But the woman was neck deep in the mafiosi, the government needed her testimony and, realistically thinking, this was an extraordinary circumstance. He needed a truce between them, so it made sense to do whatever necessary to tear down her wall of animosity. And considering his plan for getting her somewhere safe meant having a plan separate from the one he'd arranged with the special prosecutor and her lawyer, he needed that truce within the hour.

He leaned against the doorframe in order to take some weight off his sore foot. "Edwin Daly is a mafiosi informant."

"He's an assistant district attorney. He prosecutes gangsters."

Prosecution and conviction weren't the same thing, and Edwin Daly's conviction record of gangsters was small.

"I have enough evidence to arrest him, but I also want the man who has been padding his pockets."

She nodded, just nodded.

"Billy O'Flaherty."

She frowned.

"His photograph was the second in the binder. You didn't recognize him."

"Oh. Why wasn't Mr. Daly in the binder?"

"Until he's brought up on charges, he's still an assistant district attorney."

She nodded as if that made sense to her.

She was rather nice to look at, with the contrast between her amber eyes and tobacco-colored hair worn piled on top of her head like a crown. A few strands grazed the part of her collarbone exposed by the wide neckline of her gown. Frank swallowed and returned his attention to her face. But it wasn't merely those details that he found attractive. She didn't lower her lids like a coquette. He'd noticed how she met Cady's gaze with the same boldness as she met his, which was how she had also looked at Edwin Daly. Malia Vaccarelli wasn't timid and insecure, which some men wouldn't admire, but he did. He liked confident women, and when they were in lacy gowns that accentuated every feminine curve...

Frank cleared his throat. "I'm sorry you are caught up in this."

She nodded again, just nodded.

"I'm not what you think I am," he insisted. "Give me the benefit of the doubt."

"And put my life at risk?"

"If I wanted you dead, we wouldn't be speaking now."

She opened her mouth then closed it.

Frank sighed. It'd been a long day, his foot was aching, he'd missed lunch and he didn't care much for the musty smell inside the train car from the last passengers, but this conversation needed to happen now. "May I ask how it is you have such a negative view of law enforcement personnel?"

Her eyes flared. "Coppers beat my grandfather until he learned to speak to them in English," she snapped, her beauty unblemished by the accusatory edge in her words.

"Coppers beat my father until he paid for their protection. Weekly they collected donations from his businesses."

"Is it possible," he said softly, "that your father and grandfather did not share the whole truth regarding those events? That maybe they were beaten for mafiosi involvement? The donations were really payoffs?"

She shifted uncomfortably, and when she spoke, her jaw barely moved. "Yes."

He didn't fault her for resenting his question. Nor did her animosity bother him. If he were in her shoes, he'd be as suspicious, angry and embarrassed as she was. Not to mention exhausted. But he couldn't leave his questioning there. He had to push her into reevaluating what she'd been taught, so that she would open her mind to viewing him as her protector.

He ensured his tone stayed gentle. "In light of that, is it possible they were erroneous about all police being corrupt?" When she didn't answer, he asked again, "Could they have been?"

"Yes," she bit off. "Is that what you want to hear? You're right, I'm wrong. You're honorable, I'm debased. You're—" Her voice broke; eyes welled with tears. She turned to the mirror, gripped the sink, her shoulders shaking as she cried. "I don't know what…is wrong with…me. This isn't— I don't cry. I don't yell at strangers…or friends… or family…or anyone at all."

That didn't surprise him. Anne Morgan had, indeed, described Miss Vaccarelli as a kindhearted soul, without an enemy in the world, someone able to put the most unfriendly sort at ease. Yet she looked battle-weary.

"You've had a rough day," he offered.

She wiped her eyes, smearing the soot from her fingers onto her skin. "Oh, splendid."

The train's whistle blew and the train started to move forward to where they would pick up passengers. That meant he had only a specific amount of time in his metaphorical hourglass to reach that truce. Or else she wouldn't get off the train with him. That then would mean he would have to toss her over his shoulder and carry her off, literally speaking.

Frank withdrew a handkerchief from his coat pocket and offered it to her. "Here."

She took it with a whispered, "Thank you."

He wasn't one to take advantage of an injury, but he suspected she needed an excuse to sit down. Only her need to look strong would never admit it.

"My broken toe is screaming for me to give it a rest." Not necessarily a lie because his foot was aching. He took a step back then motioned to the seating area. "Would you mind if we continued this conversation over there? Please?"

# *Chapter 6*

One might say the perfect traveler is one whose digestion is perfect, whose disposition is cheerful, who can be enthusiastic under the most discouraging circumstances.

—Emily Price Post, *Etiquette*

Frank waited until Miss Vaccarelli passed him, then he followed her to the seating area near the front of the car. She sat on the edge of the sofa, clutching a fringed velvet pillow to her stomach as if it were a shield, leaving him the chairs to choose from. Frank sank into the chair to her left, the better of the two to give him a view of the locked door. No one was expected to enter, at least not until they made it to New Rochelle. Still, he kept a gun within easy reach. If he were at home, he'd prop his foot up on the table; at his office, up on a stool. Here he had to make do with extending his leg in front of him.

"How's your arm?" It was an abrupt restart to their conversation, but it was superficial, inoffensive and, now that Frank thought of it, something he actually wanted to know.

She looked from one arm to the other then back at him. "They're fine. Why do you ask?"

"Cady grabbed you pretty hard."

Her lips formed an O. She touched the spot where Cady's fist had clenched. "It doesn't feel bruised."

"Good. If it bruises, let me know."

"And what will you do about it if it does? Demand a duel with the special prosecutor?"

That her expression was as serious as her tone caused Frank pause. So far in their short acquaintance, she'd shown no predilection toward sarcasm or a dry wit. Yet...

"I was thinking ice pack." And then, because he couldn't help himself: "But if a duel would please you more, mi-lady, I'll have one arranged."

"I'm Van Kelly's sister." She said it in the same manner one would say, *I'm King Herod's wife. I deserve neither pity nor mercy.*

He touched the arm of the sofa, leaning forward. "No woman deserves a bruise." He stared at her long enough for her to see he was deathly serious.

Something flickered in her eyes. A hint of gratitude, perhaps, but he hoped it was something more, such as the bud of an epiphany that he wasn't the heathen she'd presumed him to be. Or something resembling a simple *You're a good man, Frank Louden.*

The train slowed, brakes squealing, and the whistle blew again. They were approaching the loading platform, where hundreds would pile into the Shore Line Express for the multitude of stops between here and Boston.

Frank eased back in his chair to give her needed space. Making her nervy would counter his progress, and he didn't have time to tear down that wall a second time. "When people marry," he said, "they don't inherently trust one another."

Her head tilted, and he could practically see the interest she had in what he would say next. Not all women were like that. Some didn't want to spend an evening by the fire, just the two of them and a conversation. Some didn't enjoy conversation…or, at least, not conversation with him. Some despised watching those stupid baseball games at the Polo Grounds. They wanted to go only to operas, symphonies and balls, which he didn't mind attending. Relationships should be give-and-take, not all take.

"You were saying?" she put in.

Frank started at her voice, so lost in his thoughts. "Saying?"

"When people marry…?"

The train continued to slow, brakes squealing; tracks rattled underneath them, vibrating the floor. The whistle repeatedly blew. With the private coach still in the tunnel, no one could see them, no one would know they were here, unless someone came looking.

Frank shifted on his seat as his mind scrambled to remember his point. "When people marry, both partners choose to give the other the benefit of the doubt because they're in love. As long as the benefit of the doubt is not destroyed, time and experience allow trust to grow. Our situation is similar even though the relationship is platonic."

She was watching him with a curious expression. "Go on."

"You've had twenty-five years of being taught one thing—law enforcement personnel are all corrupt. I can't change your mind-set after only a few hours of our knowing each other." She opened her mouth to speak, and Frank rushed out with, "It's not a criticism, Miss Vaccarelli. I'm as much a creature of habit, upbringing and prejudices as you are, as anyone is. And not all habits, upbringing or prejudices are bad."

Her lips pursed a bit. "I am not all you think I am either."

That he doubted. She was as unveiled as they came.

He leaned forward, elbows on knees, fingers steepled together to form a hollow triangle. "All I ask is that you give me the benefit of the doubt until I can prove to you I'm trustworthy. I will extend the same to you." He held her gaze, hoping she would see the sincerity in his eyes matched his tone. He didn't know why her thinking favorably of him mattered, but it did. "Surely I've given you some reason to believe something good about me," he said with a chuckle.

Her shoulders tightened; head shook.

Frank bit back from sharing the half dozen reasons that sprang to his mind. Twenty-five years had built a stronghold in her mind. He shouldn't expect loosening a stone would be easy. "No offense taken. Would it be easier for you to list what I've done to justify your doubts regarding my good intentions?"

Her fingers nervously plucked at her skirt as they had in Cady's office.

Frank shifted in his chair. Her discomfort was palpable. He could see in her body language her internal battle over how to respond. Change was hard enough without someone forcing you do it. He abhorred change himself, at least the kind thrust upon him by people seeking the best only for themselves. Contrary to what she believed, once she testified at the deposition, she wasn't going back to her cozy Waldorf apartment and volunteering at the Museum of Art. In three weeks, Malia Vaccarelli would be dead. Explaining that to her would have to wait.

They sat for another minute or so.

She exhaled. Then she looked at him. "Mr. Louden, you

evaluated me correctly in that I do like to have my own way. I can be terribly selfish." She turned her face toward the coach's front entrance. He could see only her profile. "Compounding the matter is that I've known for years the degree of my depravity. It is a battle I've yet to win."

He understood. Selfishness infected him too, pointed out by every significant person in his life. But if a man wanted to climb a mountain, win a race, develop a successful invention, he had to make decisions for his best interest. What could a man accomplish if in all things he behaved selflessly and allowed others to move ahead of him in line? Starvation. Poverty. Last-place ribbon. A future processing evidence. The list could go on.

Frank grinned to lighten the mood, even though she wasn't looking his way. "Selfishness isn't the most appealing trait, but one I can relate to. I don't fault you for taking the most comfortable seat in the coach, but be warned, if you leave it, it's mine."

She turned, gazing at him in confusion. "How is it you gained this epiphany about trust?"

"Personal experience."

Pink tinged her cheeks. "I didn't realize you were married."

Frank walked to the side window and stared at the tunnel wall, the brick blackened with soot. So many safe, useless conversations they could be having, and yet Miss Vaccarelli ignored those in lieu of this one. In the windowpane he could see her reflection. She sat there, serenely, with her elegant hands folded in her lap, beckoning him to share his darkest secrets. It seemed the most natural thing in the world—their talking together.

"I was married," he admitted, "for six months and fourteen days."

Her lips parted with surprise. "I'm so sorry. Death is

heartbreaking, and even more so when a loved one dies young."

Frank released a wry chuckle. In a month, they would never see each other again. She didn't need to know. He didn't need to tell her, nor was he under any moral or ethical obligation to. Yet the words were there, already, on his tongue, waiting for breath to give them life. His heart pounded in nervous anticipation. The overwhelming need to confess to her was strange because he didn't know her. He didn't, but it felt as if he did.

"I'm divorced."

"That must not have been an easy decision," she answered without pause, or any judgmental underlying.

"For me, yes. She had no qualms." Frank turned to face her, and with his hands behind his back, he leaned against the coach wall. The wood paneling vibrated against his palms. "I was twenty-two and didn't know how to be the husband she wanted."

"I'm sorry," was all she said.

"Don't be. Rose found another husband, and I found Jesus." He let out a chuckle. "I say my life turned out for the better."

She looked at him as if she wasn't sure what to make of his comment.

"You can ask me anything," he offered.

"My curiosity is piqued, as anyone's would be, but it would be too forward to ask personal questions on such a short acquaintance."

"Your response wounds me."

Her brows rose, and he'd swear she was smiling—almost—because he knew he was.

"Yes, you do indeed look to be in pain," she answered, and as he laughed, she continued on. "You must have marshally things to attend to, so I will leave you to court your melancholy." Her gaze shifted from him to the table between the sofa and the chair. From the small stack, she claimed a book with a familiar green cover, opened it and began to read. Or at least pretend as if she was reading *Dorothy lived in the midst of the great Kansas prairies…*

Frank moved from the side wall to the connecting entrance to stand guard. Their conversation couldn't end. Not like that.

"Miss Vaccarelli?"

She looked up. Her pink lips curved enough to count as a smile…on the *Mona Lisa*. "Yes?"

"I confided about being divorced because I want you to know you aren't the only one with something in your life of which you're ashamed." He paused. "As a sworn officer of the law, I will give up my life to keep you safe. That's the truth whether you trust me to do it or not."

She nodded. He turned back to the coach door to listen. All he heard was her charming sigh and then her decidedly sociable voice. "Mr. Louden?"

"Yes?"

"Is this what Generals Lee and Grant felt like at Appomattox?"

The train whistled and started forward.

Frank looked over his shoulder. Her eyes, which had been so accusatory and antagonistic before, were softer. Kind. His feet itched to move back to the chair, to continue their conversation about him, about her, about the art exhibit this morning, if she wanted. Since making eye contact at the hotel, he had wanted to get to know her. Still did. But he held his ground because he was a marshal and she was a witness.

"It's either a truce," he said, offering her his most disarming smile, "or we've both passed out from starvation."

Her lips twitched, he hoped, in amusement. "I choose your protection."

That stunned him. "You don't have a choice."

The corner of her mouth eased upward. She gave him a look, one that needed no interpreting, but one quite familiar. He did, after all, have a mother, two grandmothers, four aunts, a sister, three wise-beyond-their-years (so they claimed) nieces and scores of female friends and acquaintances. None of them, though, appealed to him on the level this one did. Now that she wasn't looking at him in hopes he'd fall off the face of the earth, her eyes reminded him of his grandfather's prized cognac, imported from France and selfishly unshared. And that dot to the right of the center of her lips called forth all the wonders of her face.

She turned her attention to the book.

Her smug grin was one Frank was glad he couldn't see anymore. Keeping her alive, he could do. Ensuring he didn't do something foolish yet typical to those of his gender...

*Approximately thirty minutes later*

Brakes squeaked, the whistle screeched and the train slowed.

Malia turned to the next engrossing page in *The Wonderful Wizard of Oz.* New Rochelle was the first stop outside New York City. On a shelf in her bedroom were four empty commutation ticket books that used to contain sixty passages between the two cities, leftover souvenirs from her years at Vassar. The station was nowhere near as interesting as poor little Dorothy alone among those strange people of Oz with nothing to protect her but a round shining mark on her forehead by the Witch of the North.

It'd taken her several minutes to start reading because questions about Mr. Louden had flooded her mind. But once she entered the world L. Frank Baum had created, she soaked in every word. She should have bought the book a year ago, when it was first published.

"Miss Vaccarelli?"

Malia reluctantly looked up, closing the book but holding her place in chapter four with her thumb. He lounged in his chair with his legs crossed, while she, as dictated by Society, was allowed less freedom of posture. Back straight, shoulders erect, long neck high, hands elegantly posed. Every moment of a lady must be full of grace and dignity, while a man could nurse his foot if he pleased. What she'd give to kick off her shoes or flop onto her stomach as she read.

Mr. Louden leaned forward in his chair, his hat fitted snugly atop his wheat-blond hair, his pocket watch in hand. His eyes—as blue as the houses, clothes, sheets and rugs in Munchkin land—were watching her with such concern. And she felt— She felt— Her skin prickled with awareness. She couldn't breathe. It was as if they were back at the hotel. That moment when it'd felt as if they were the only two people in the courtyard. The moment—seconds, really—stretched for hours. She expected him to wink, as one of the Scarecrow's eyes had winked at Dorothy. He didn't.

"Did you speak?" she asked, then cringed at the inanity of the question from a brain still stuck in a book. She corrected with: "I mean, you were saying?"

He closed the lid of his watch with a click.

"I'm playing a game of odds." His voice was devoid of its earlier levity, now sounding as it had in the special prosecutor's office—work-focused. "Considering the precautions I took to get you on the Shore Line Express, the odds are mafiosi thugs aren't also on the train. However, too many people in Cady's office knew of the plan to take you to Boston, double back and then continue on to Long Island. I'm not willing to gamble that someone won't squeal, either willingly or by force."

"By 'force,' you mean 'beaten until confession'?" Malia returned, expecting his answer yet hoping he wouldn't say—

"Yes."

She closed her eyes. This couldn't be happening. But it was, and she could no longer ignore the reality of the world the cyclone named Giovanni had spun her into. She met his gaze again. "Then Irene is in danger because of me."

"I'm sorry." He actually looked apologetic. "The moment you stepped inside Cady's office, you put them all in danger." He slid his watch into a vest pocket. "Word will get around, if it hasn't already, of what you've done. You made yourself an even greater target. Someone who wants to find you will track every person you spoke with today, beginning with Edwin Daly. Desperate men aren't gentlemen to women with information."

The train jolted to a stop.

Malia stared at the book cover; the image of the Tin Man and Scarecrow blurred. So desperate to rescue Giovanni and do the honorable thing, she'd never considered how her actions would affect others. Her throat burned with something acerbic and foul, condemning and true: she'd been—still was—disgustingly naive.

"If anything bad happens to Irene, Miss Barn, or" —her voice quavered— "anyone who knows me, I will never be able to forgive myself."

"I can't imagine you would," he murmured.

"What's that mean?"

"Kindhearted people assume burdens not their own."

Malia's eyes widened. She bit back her response, unsure if she was complimented or insulted, or both.

He slid the book out of her hands and rested it on the table with the others. "This is our stop."

Malia looked longingly at the book. "We're supposed to go to Boston."

"Yes, we were." He said nothing more as he walked to the back of the coach and reclaimed her traded straw hat and trench coat. His silence gave her time to think, because…because he wanted her to reason it all out on her own? That could mean he believed she was capable of putting the pieces together. After the day she'd had, she needed a chance to show she wasn't obtuse, not for his benefit, but because he'd known she needed to prove it to herself.

"This was your plan all along—deboarding at New Rochelle."

He walked back to her. "Why do you think that?"

Malia stood and allowed him to help her into the coat. "If the mafiosi questions Irene, Cady or anyone in his offices, everyone can convincingly speak the truth because that is the truth they know. So presuming no mafiosi thugs followed us to the train, if they find out about our plans, it would make sense for them to wait in Grand Central for us to return."

Her reasoning made sense, and must have been in line with his because he didn't answer. She'd promised herself she'd give him the benefit of the doubt until he gave her cause not to trust him. Now was the moment to take a step of faith.

She turned to face him. "Where is the yellow brick road leading us?"

He planted the hat atop her head, but because of the Apollo knot she'd twisted her hair into, the hat didn't sit level. He lifted it off. "To wear or not to wear—that is the question."

Malia looked up at him and couldn't help smiling. He was a hand's length taller than Mr. Daly, and taller than her brother too. He was more likable when he was being jovial Frank Louden than stoic Deputy Marshal Louden.

She took the hat from him. "To answer or not answer—that is what you've been avoiding."

He chuckled. "That didn't quite make sense."

Malia shrugged. She'd never boasted of having the cleverest of wits.

"It's nice to see you this way." He began to button her coat—from bottom to top—as Giovanni used to do when they were children before they ran off for an afternoon of play in Central Park.

"What way?"

"Smiling. Relaxed."

She supposed she was relaxed. Reading had soothed her spirit and taken her mind off her troubles. "I've done enough crying."

He paused on the last button, the one at the collar. "You don't deserve the situation your brother has put you in." He lowered his hands but didn't step back.

She'd been closer to a man, dancing at a ball and amid the huddled masses leaving the opera, but it'd never—never—felt like this. She could smell him, feel his closeness. She should be fearful and wary of this stranger who had invaded her life and, even more so, the bubble of space around her. But she wasn't fearful. Or wary. For the first time since she received word of her parents' and nonni's deaths, she didn't quite feel so alone.

"Whether I deserve this situation or not," she said, "bemoaning will change nothing. I may as well make the best of my circumstances."

He nudged her into motion to the door. "Not many people would have had the courage or rectitude to do what you did." He flashed a smile that made her feel warm everywhere. "Even fewer would have the pluck to set aside ingrained fears and place her life in another's hands."

He believed that about her?

She intended to say "thank you" but instead blurted, "That you were checking your watch leads me to wonder if the time is significant."

He pulled his pocket watch out long enough to check the hour. "It's now quarter after five."

Malia paused as he unlocked the coach door and opened it a crack to look outside. "Sunset is at six-thirty," she said. "It'll be dark by seven. Are we taking the trolley to Glen Island?"

He shook his head. "You need to do exactly what I say."

## *Chapter 7*

[If], when she alights at her destination, her friends
fail to meet her, she should on no account accept a
stranger's offer, whether man or woman, to deliver
her to her destination. The safest thing to do is to
walk.

—Emily Price Post, *Etiquette*

Frank kept his gaze casual as they strolled like strangers
across the station's wooden floor. With Miss Vaccarelli two
steps in front of him, as he instructed, they were far enough
apart to not look to be together, yet close enough that he
could come to her aid if need be. His heart thudded in his
chest, his nerves on edge. Upward of a hundred people were
in the New Rochelle station lobby. Yet not a single person
loitering near the plaster walls, at the ticket counter or on the
benches looked suspicious. Nor was anyone trailing them.

He hated when things were easy. Not because they were

harbingers of eventual woes—even though a fraction of the time they were—but mostly because when it was over, he ended up kicking himself over making a mountain out of a molehill.

Miss Vaccarelli walked with elegance, maneuvering through the crowd; one hand held her straw hat, the other halfway inside the coat's outer pocket. Occasionally a man would give her an admiring glance. When she paid him no notice, he returned to his book, newspaper or conversation. All was going smoothly until a man with superb whiskers and a velvet morning coat stepped in front of her.

Miss Vaccarelli stopped.

A hurried couple and their gaggle of children and luggage blocked Frank from her.

The man shifted his cane to his left hand, took off his hat with his right, and shifted his hat to his left hand, as well. "I think you dropped this," he said, offering a glove that seemed to come out of nowhere.

Miss Vaccarelli looked at the man in surprise. "Thank you, but it's not mine. If you would excuse me, I must be going."

"My apologies." He didn't move. "Lovely weather, isn't it?"

Her fingers tightened around her hat's brim. "Why, yes, it—"

"Leah? Leah Carr?" Frank put in the moment his path was clear.

She glanced over her shoulder—and in that split second, he'd swear her eyes sparkled in delight upon seeing him. No woman had ever looked at him as if he was her knight in shining armor. She did. More so, he felt like it.

Then she gasped in a manner fitting her impromptu performance, whirling around to face him. "Frank Marshall?" she said, all sweetness and light. "Good heavens, is it really you?"

"In the flesh." He walked to her. "How do you do?"

"Splendid. And you?"

He glanced at the stranger and lifted his hat slightly, before returning his attention to Miss Vaccarelli. "What are you doing in New Rochelle?"

"I'm here to surprise my grandfather."

He gave her a taken-aback look. "I thought you two weren't on speaking terms."

She laughed. "That's why this is a surprise."

After she politely wished the whiskered man a good afternoon, Frank walked with her to the door, saying, "We're celebrating my cousin's birthday at Besly's Tavern. Johnny thinks I'm…"

They continued the meaningless yet friendly chatter all the way out of the building.

Frank moved to the curbside of the pavement. The trolley bell clanged. He placed a hand on her lower back and nudged her past the commuters home from New York City and waiting to board the trolley. They continued down the covered walkway, passing by the horse-drawn carriages.

"You handled that well," he said, looking around to find their ride. "Might I say you know how to not panic."

"Thank you, kind sir," answered Miss Vaccarelli with a slight curtsy.

Ah, there was Norma, sitting in her girlie electric runabout, the first of six automobiles parked at the station. He returned his attention to Miss Vaccarelli, who was now looking around, observing her surroundings, checking to see, as had he, if anyone was following them. She figured out on her own to do that. It rather impressed him. She was clever and teachable, and he liked that—he liked her—more than he ought to.

A train whistle blew. An engine began to pull away from the station, rolling past them on the left.

"Confess," he said over the clackety-clack of the loco-motive. "You have a secret life on the stage, don't you?"

"Well, I didn't want to say anything, but…" She turned enough for him to see the mischievousness in her eyes. "In my acting debut at Grace Church, I played the baby Jesus. Apparently, I captured the essence of 'no crying he made.'"

He made his expression grave. "That takes skill, for I know very few babies who don't excel in wailing. I, my-self, was a renowned wailer."

Her brows rose. "That sounds exhausting."

"My parents said so."

"I imagine they would."

"My offspring, I fear, will be as vocally endowed."

"Their mother will be most appreciative." Then she shrugged modestly. "Alas, my predilection for silence drew such acclaim that my managers insisted I retire. Once one reaches the pinnacle, the only place to go is down. Or so was reported in the *Times* in explaining the next Christ-mas to disgruntled fans why I wasn't chosen to play a na-tivity goat."

"No," he protested. He placed a hand over his heart. "A gifted performer's career cut short before her time. Oh the indignities! I am in despair."

Malia looked at him, at the lightheartedness brightening his face, and she couldn't maintain a faux solemnity. She smiled. True, it showed only on her lips, but she felt it—verily felt it—to the tips of her toes. It felt good to laugh, to be merry and silly and absurd, and pretend they were other people. People who didn't live in fear or pursuit of the mafiosi. She hadn't laughed since her parents died. She'd buried a part of herself with them, and Giovanni hadn't minded—or maybe he hadn't noticed—her grief, her lifelessness. Her facade.

But this man made her remember what it was like to

enjoy life. She didn't want to lose that again. She didn't want to return to being dull, dutiful Malia.

"Well, now," a female voice broke the companionable silence, "aren't you two chummy?"

Malia stopped abruptly and jerked her gaze to a towering woman standing next to a fancy red-wheeled electric automobile. Her black hip-length, three-button coat notched at the lapel, skirt with matching buttons, and white blouse with a necktie and standing collar all appeared expertly tailored. White kid gloves. Small beaded purse with chain handle. Silk rose-topped hat. Whoever she was, because of her abnormal height, her attire could not have come off a rack at B. Altman's, Macy's or Gimbels. It most likely was sewn by the exclusive ladies' tailor at Lord and Taylor.

Yet for all her femininity and sophistication…

On her left lapel was a marshal's badge, an exact replica of the one Mr. Louden had placed in his inner coat pocket moments before they'd stepped outside Special Prosecutor Cady's office building. Resting at her hip was a holstered gun. Languishing in her eyes was the knowledge and confidence to use it.

The trolley bell rang again.

Malia glanced over her shoulder to see it leaving the station.

"Good to see you, Norma." Mr. Louden put his hand under Malia's elbow and assisted her off the curb. He stepped to the vehicle, and Malia followed. Gone was his smile. In its place was the dour marshal expression. "Miss Vaccarelli, this is Miss Norma Hogan, deputy marshal Southern District of New York."

They clasped hands, gave them a dropping movement rather than a shake, then let go.

"It's very good of you to help us," Miss Hogan said in a chipper tone.

Malia nodded since she wasn't sure of a fitting response, yet it seemed she should at least acknowledge the friendly comment.

Mr. Louden asked, "Why didn't Winslow come with you?"

An awkward pause, then: "Someone called requesting help, so he went." Miss Hogan snatched a leather-bound notebook off the black padded seat. "Now, then, we need to get you two on your way." She gave Mr. Louden the notebook. "You *will* follow my rules of usage. All of them. Properly. To a tee."

He didn't say anything. He didn't turn his head to look Malia's way, or acknowledge Miss Hogan's comments with a polite nod. Whatever he was thinking distracted him.

She wasn't at all certain that was a good thing.

"*Ehrm,* Frank," was all Miss Hogan got out before he said, "Yes, ma'am." He opened the notebook, eyes scanning the first page. "Oh, come on, Norma. This is beyond what's necessary. Is this because I told Winslow you think he's cute?"

"Winslow is a—" She snatched the booklet back. "You offended Dee Dee on the day I first showed her to you by calling her a 'woman's car.' Even though I love you like a brother—or, at the bare minimum, like the coworker who annoys me the least—I am under no obligation to allow you to borrow her for three weeks outside my parental eye."

He looked to Malia. "You're a woman. Tell her she's being ridiculous."

She could. She probably ought to, but in that moment nothing appealed to her less. Who knew a man's duress could be so gratifying to watch.

Malia cringed apologetically even though she didn't feel it a bit. "Sorry. Miss Hogan does have a point."

"A point?" He uttered one of those I'm-trying-to-be-patient-with-you noises that men utter when they believe they are being patient but any female could tell they had long lost patience. "Norma is a woman, and it's her automobile. *Aught. Tow. Mo. Bill,*" he repeated in that patronizing manner while still looking at Malia yet motioning to Miss Hogan to give him back the booklet, which she didn't.

"How," he continued, "is calling something what it is offensive?"

"I'm a woman," Miss Hogan said, and one corner of her mouth slid into a wry curve, "and it would be highly offensive for you to call me 'Woman' when, in fact, I do have a name."

His face screwed up.

"As Dee Dee does," Miss Hogan declared.

A snort escaped Malia's lips. She covered her mouth with the brim of her hat.

He glared at her then turned it upon Miss Hogan. "It's a car, not a person."

"It's quite common to name a horse," Malia said in Miss Hogan's defense.

"That's not the same," he answered.

Miss Hogan's eyes narrowed to slits. "Frank Louden, you are—" She coughed a breath. "Cordelia 'Dee Dee' Hogan is not a mere car. She is a Packard Model C runabout with a 183.8 cubic-inch engine capable of producing 12 horsepower and reaching 40 miles per hour. She is the tenth car James Ward Packard produced this year. She has a removable dos-a-dos rear seat, sits atop a 76-inch wheelbase, features an H-pattern gear change and steering wheel and column in a day when most other marques are still using a tiller, and—AND—*and,* all of her loveliness can be purchased from the factory for only $1,500. Like Eve at creation, she is nothing short of remarkable."

Mr. Louden snatched the booklet back. "Fine."

Deep dimples appeared on each side of Miss Hogan's mouth. "Dee Dee's batteries need proper charging every fifty-seven miles. A second set of charged batteries is in the compartment under the seat, if you need them. However, she prefers the first set to be recharged because she says the backup set doesn't feel like they fit as well as the first ones do."

"Vehicles don't have feelings," he muttered. "Or talk."

Malia leaned against him and whispered, "You shouldn't have said that so loudly. I'm sure Dee Dee heard."

He gave her a sideways look. "It's an inanimate object."

Malia held a finger up to her lips. "Shh." Then she looked to Miss Hogan. "When a man hasn't eaten in hours, his mind..." She grimaced, waved in a circular motion at the air around her forehead and said no more.

Mr. Louden's mouth hung open.

"Understandable," retorted Miss Hogan. "Now Frank, never—*never*—never take Dee Dee out for a drive without first ensuring her batteries are fully and properly charged. And it is imperative you charge the batteries after using her."

"My brother owns a petromobile," Malia said in a dry tone. "Between the smell, noise and vibration, it's quite unpleasant to ride in. I named it Prince Camel."

"That's clever," Miss Hogan said.

Mr. Louden regarded her unblinking. "Vehicles don't need names."

Miss Hogan looked as if she was trying not to laugh. And that's when Malia knew. The man, too much, liked having his own way. A creature of habit, upbringing and prejudices, he was. This was about getting Frank Louden to go above and beyond merely for the sake of making someone he cared about happy.

"Mr. Louden," Malia interjected, "while emotions dictate otherwise, need and want are not the same." She took much pleasure in the fact he appeared at a loss as to how to respond. Emboldened, she said, "I like the way you think, Miss Hogan."

"I like you, too, Miss Vaccarelli," Miss Hogan said. "Keep her alive, Frank, or I will make your life unbearable."

Mr. Louden opened his mouth. "You already—"

And she shushed him. "It's bad form to air differences."

He turned to the next page in the notebook, head shaking, not saying anything.

Miss Hogan went on, "You will bathe Dee Dee in the morning after each use, using a towel of Egyptian cotton in a clockwise motion to dry her. While it may seem prudent to leave the drying to the sun, kill that thought, for the sun leaves spots."

"No woman likes to be spotty," Malia put in.

Mr. Louden rolled his eyes.

Undismayed, Miss Hogan continued on with, "Also, oil her bearings using the specified viscosity, lubricant and amount listed. Her tires must be pumped to one hundred and twenty-five pounds to the square inch, and don't forget—"

"Norma," Mr. Louden cut in, holding the booklet up, "I can read. I'd also like to reach our destination before sunset."

A blush stole across her cheeks. "Of course." She turned to the side and dusted the black leather seat. "Be a good girl. Mommy will see you in three weeks."

Whatever Mr. Louden's thoughts, he didn't vocalize them. He put his hand under Malia's elbow and assisted her into the cab. Malia scooted over to the right side. Since the folding hood was up, she wedged the straw hat between her thigh and the side wall. Mr. Louden settled in next to her and started up the car.

Miss Hogan back-stepped until she found purchase

under the covered walkway. "On the rear seat," she called out, "is a basket with food from Besly's Tavern."

"Excellent." He shifted into reverse and looked over his shoulder, backing up.

Malia caught Miss Hogan's gaze and returned a smug grin. "I'll ensure he reads and follows the booklet."

Miss Hogan waved.

"You do know how to drive this," Malia said at a level only Mr. Louden could hear.

"My grandmother has a Studebaker."

"My fears are assuaged."

"My pleasure." He stopped and shifted into first.

Malia waved at Miss Hogan, who waved back.

"So, Mr. Louden, what is this Emerald City to which we are headed?" she asked as the car moved from the gravel lot and onto the street, the cobblestones making for bumpy progress.

"Tuxedo," he answered.

Malia's mouth gaped. His mention of Tuxedo Park was a jest. Had to be. Everyone knew Tuxedo was a colony of ultraexclusive wealthy people who lived in luxurious houses and entertained lavishly. They didn't welcome outsiders.

She knew because, back in '88, Grandfather DeWitt's quest to purchase land was rebuffed by the Tuxedo Park Association, under the auspices of Pierre Lorillard and his heirs. In retaliation, Grandfather had written a letter to the *Times* clarifying that Cora Urquhart Brown Potter, Lorillard's mistress at the time, had originated the brilliant idea, not Lorillard, to turn the useless game park into a playground for his friends and cohorts. Malia's thirteenth birthday party had been ruined because Grandfather could talk of nothing else except "that philanderer Lorillard." Even after her debut into Society, Malia had never received an invitation into the community. Even to visit.

Mr. Louden stopped at the first intersection. A horse-drawn carriage pulled to Malia's side of the car, bringing with it the aroma of equine and manure. They waited for the pedestrian traffic to cross North Street.

"Your excitement is intoxicating," he said.

"People don't go into Tuxedo whenever they like. Not even the U.S. Marshal Service has free access."

He shrugged as if to say that was no concern of his.

His action only inflamed her more. In his naive attempt to enter the park, he would humiliate them both. She had to warn him. She had to make him understand the folly of his actions.

"Mr. Louden, that eight-foot barbed wire fence around the park is there not to keep people in. Eight. Feet," she stressed. "Barbed wire. Keep out."

His frown was evident even though his gaze stayed on the road. "Out?"

"Yes, as in...we don't want you in."

"Oh. Ooohhh."

She smiled—well, smirked—at him. If felt good to be right in something.

"I can get us in," he boasted.

"Were you not listening?"

"If I remember correctly, my grandparents have a house there and I haven't been barred from visiting." He grimaced. "Yet."

Grandparents?

Malia held her breath in shock, in refusal to believe what her ears knew they heard. Her mind, though, shuddered through memories from the day. There was something she'd missed, something she had to remember, something in the law library. That vague memory, the one of Irene introducing Van Wyck Cady and Frank...

Grahame Louden.

Malia gasped in air.

As in, the grandson of the esteemed Charles and Jo-sephine Grahame, who lived on Millionaire's Row, and second son to Henry and Anne Louden of the Newport Loudens, who repeatedly were mentioned in the society column for their philanthropic and political donations. No wonder Anne Morgan had greeted him so fondly. And the Goulds, for that matter. If Josephine White Grahame was indeed his grandmother, then that made him second cousin twice removed to Lina Schermerhorn Astor. Good thing Malia was already sitting.

What was she to say? She didn't know what to say. She had to say something in response. She couldn't go into Tuxedo. For heaven's sake, the hem of her dress was more gray than white.

And then, the moment she noticed her hands trembling, a trolley bell rang a block away. Malia flinched. The horse-drawn carriage turned right onto the paved North Street. Mr. Louden eased the car into the intersection and turned left, shifting into the next gear. It increased speed as it took them north.

On her right, a darkening sky. On her left, above the trees and buildings, the sun painted streaks of red and pink amid the blue. Wasn't Tuxedo forty miles from New Rochelle? If they made Tuxedo by sunset, they would be fortunate.

They passed several buildings, automobiles, carriages, pedestrians and a park.

She cleared her dry throat.

"For what reason," Malia finally began—she didn't actually believe he was being serious, did she?— "will, ah, we—and by we, I mean you—tell people we are there? In Tuxedo."

"How about…we're engaged."

She sputtered a most unladylike cough. "Engaged?" Her cheeks warmed. "I don't think that is wise."

He spared a glance in her direction. "It worked well for us in getting on the train."

"Yes, but we will never see the engineer again. And you couldn't exactly show your badge and draw attention to the fact a marshal was trying to sneak a woman on a train."

She shifted on the bench to face him, even though all it did was give her a clearer view of his profile, and that perfectly sculpted jaw with a day's growth of blond bristles. When Papà used to come home from work, she would jump into his arms and brush her palms against his bristled cheeks. For good luck, she'd say. Each time she returned home from Vassar, he intentionally skipped shaving. He'd hold her palms against his cheeks and whisper, "For good luck."

He lied to her about coppers. He was a criminal, a thief, and he'd left her an inheritance built on deception and a safe with counterfeit bills. Yet despite it all, she missed him. Some nights she missed him so that her heart physically ached. Some nights she would lie in bed, stare out her window at the stars and wish to have him and Mamma back. Some nights she pretended they were. For all of Papà's faults, he loved her. As Nonno had loved her. As Nonna. As Mamma. They had raised her with love and laughter, and the belief that she could marry for love, and she buried four empty caskets because their bodies, like their yacht, lay beneath the Atlantic.

Malia let out a long, uneven breath. She'd tried to live a God-honoring life, and look where it left her. Alone. It wasn't right. Or fair.

*I want something more, Jesus. Something different. Something abundant and true.*

She refocused her attention on Mr. Louden. "What will happen when the Tuxedo-ites hear the news of our 'engagement'? I can't imagine there isn't a grapevine there."

He seemed to give that some thought.

They passed Huguenot Lake on their left, and the road narrowed, emptied of all but them. He shifted into the next gear, increasing speed.

Malia decided to answer for him. "They will want to meet Frank Louden's fiancée, is what will happen. They will want to congratulate him and his grandparents. That will lead to invitations to brunch and afternoon tea. Even if I use a false name, someone may recognize me. Anne Morgan will recognize me. Her family has a house there. We will be questioned when our engagement announcement will be in the *Times*. I cannot think—"

His lips twitched.

Malia growled under her breath. He had been jesting all along, which she should have known. Except for when he was focused on marshally things, he took little seriously.

"You are not amusing," she pointed out, and if she didn't feel quite so foolish, she would smile as well over her silly, though realistic, avalanche of panicked thoughts. Clearly Society women frightened her more than predatory men.

She narrowed her eyes at him. "At all."

That seemed only to amuse him more. His laughter snorted out.

They passed the outskirts of New Rochelle, the forest on each side of the road growing denser.

He smiled lazily. "Fret not, Miss Vaccarelli. My grandparents are in Europe with my parents, and will not return to the country until Independence Day. They will stay in the city until autumn. What servants are on the estate will be discreet. The housekeeper can be your chaperone. As long as we stay on the property and keep to ourselves, no one will know we are there."

"No one?"

"Practically no one." He said it with such solemnity and assurance that she felt comforted. Well, dull, dutiful and ever practical Malia felt that way.

In three weeks, her life as she'd known it, according to Special Prosecutor Cady, would come to an end, whatever that meant. She would adapt, of course. She'd keep her chin high, fight the good fight, win the race. Be the good Christian girl she desperately tried to be. Because she had to. She had to manage and survive because her brother's life depended on her. He needed time to repent and change and become a man of faith. She needed him to…so that she wouldn't be alone. Because she couldn't watch another coffin sink into the earth.

A choking feeling overtook her.

Malia shifted on the bench, tucking her right leg under the left, propping her arm on the seat back. She gripped a bar on the folded hood's frame and rested her head against the cold metal as she watched the green terrain pass by. It wasn't the proper way to sit. She didn't care.

This new her—this Leah Carr as Mr. Louden had spontaneously named her—wanted to live. She wanted to live, be fun and carefree, even if for only three weeks. For that may be all the time she had left to live, if Mr. Maranzano and his mafiosi friends had their way.

Malia pushed down the choking feeling.

No matter how few or many people were on the Grahame estate, she was going to be adventurous. She would have fun.

# Chapter 8

Suitability is the test of good taste always.
 —Emily Price Post, *Etiquette*

*Grahame Estate*
*East Lake Road, Tuxedo Park*
*7:04 p.m.*

Malia stopped with Mr. Louden at the entrance to the drawing room. A white-bearded man sat in a chair reading a book. A stately woman with salt-and-peppery hair sat at a desk, her back to the entrance. Before Malia had time to blink, gasp or pose a question, Mr. Louden grabbed her arm, jerked her back behind the wall and breathed a "Shh." They rested against the rosewood wainscoting. Her heart pounded in her chest.

Malia whispered, "That doesn't look like 'no one' to me."

"I remember saying 'practically no one,'" he ground out.

"Someone sounds a bit unhappy."

He grumbled under his breath.

Malia peeked around the wall into the drawing room—
an explosion of French Renaissance and pink. A dozen, at
least, varying-height candlesticks sat on the mantel above
the massive fireplace, where a sofa and a lone chair were
placed facing it. An unaccompanied desk behind the sofa.
Two other chairs in an opposite corner on either side of a
tabled chess set. Crystal chandelier and lemon-oil lamps.
Gold-plated plaster ceiling. The walls, what little could be
seen amid the paintings and tapestries, were pink-and-gold
striped. Too much to admire meant nothing was admired.

As a whole, the well-lighted room, while elegantly and
expensively furnished, was nothing short of aesthetically
hideous.

Malia found that odd because, even though the light
from the setting sun had been meager, she'd been able to
tell that the forest surrounding the Queen Anne-style mansion was aesthetically manicured and the carriage house
in neat array, as had been every room they'd passed by or
through since the footmen and butler had met them by the
side entrance and welcomed Mr. Louden. Then the housekeeper arrived and proceeded to take Malia's hat and coat
and suggest they wait in the French drawing room while
she had rooms prepared for their visit. No mention had
been made of Mr. and Mrs. Charles Grahame being in attendance, and certainly not of them being in the French
drawing room.

Of the room's two occupants, only one was speaking.

Mr. Louden placed his hand atop Malia's head and
nudged until she scrunched down. He leaned over her to
look inside the room, his leg against her side, his face close
enough that she could hear his even breathing. Malia focused on the conversation to keep from thinking how close
his body was to hers.

"I'm telling you, Charles," said the woman Malia deduced to be his grandmother, "a new sofa would solve the problem with this room." She pushed back the rosy chintz drapes. "And curtains, new ones in silk. Yellow. You like yellow." Wearing a periwinkle and ivory-lace day dress, the elegant woman looked no more out of place in the pink room than the framed nymphs above a Marcantonio Raimondi engraving that hung between the two towering windows. Short, straight-backed, with prominent regular features, Mrs. Grahame looked every inch an aristocrat.

The man Malia guessed was Mr. Louden's grandfather used one foot to remove a shoe then repeated the action on the other, in the same manner her shoe-abhorring Nonna used to do. He propped his socked feet on a stool, the wooden top covered with embroidery, the design Malia couldn't see. A big man physically, like his grandson, he contrasted with the slender porcelain, gold and black nymphs—three feet tall down to three inches—in the gaudy room.

Without raising his eyes from the book he held, the cover Malia also couldn't see, he grumbled, "I'm not spending another dime on another decorator to redesign this room again. Twice in thirteen years is enough."

"But—"

"No, Josie. Find a better way to fix the issue you have."

"This could be a problem," Mr. Louden murmured.

"Could be?" Malia straightened and bumped her head into his chin. She swirled around, grabbing his lapels to steady him. "Sorry."

He rubbed his chin. "You have a hard head."

She rubbed the back of her head. "You have an even harder jaw." Malia peeked around the wall again to see if the older couple had heard them. The pair was busy bickering, or at least Mrs. Grahame was. Mr. Graham's book held his attention. A cream-and-white Pomeranian jumped out of its wicker basket beside the hearth and darted underneath the sofa.

She turned back to Mr. Louden. "You said they were in Europe."

"They were." He gave her a sheepish look. "My grandfather is seventy-six. I suspect he caught an ailment that necessitated an early return."

"He looks robust."

"He tends to make an amazing recovery once he's back in New York." He straightened his suit, brushing any remaining dust from the sleeves and front. "Follow my lead."

He took a step. Malia placed a hand on his chest, stopping him.

She reached inside his coat pocket and withdrew the star-shaped badge with Deputy U.S. Marshal engraved into it. "I enjoyed pretending we were different people in New Rochelle, but I need you to be candid with them, as you have been with me." She pinned it on his left lapel then took a step back. "They're your grandparents, Mr. Louden. Treat them with honor and respect, and tell them who is seeking sanctuary in their home."

His hands rested on the hilt of each gun. "What makes you think I wouldn't be honest?" His blue eyes, intense and studious, met hers. They neither flickered nor blinked. "What are you afraid of?"

Her heart pinched. She was afraid of too much.

Malia looked away, fearful of what he might see. Even more fearful of what he might force her to confront. "They're your family. I couldn't forgive myself if they were hurt because of me."

It wasn't the proper thing. Frank knew it. He also knew when a woman needed comforting, and this one screamed with need, so he wrapped his arms around her, holding her close. She tensed, trembled. She smelled of soot and dust. And it was all because of him.

He released a weary breath and rested his chin on her crown of hair. He'd had no choice, though. He had to sneak her out of Cady's office and onto the train. He had to get her off the train in New Rochelle. He had to drive her to Tuxedo because this was the safest place for her to be. He'd done it all for her. To keep her alive. And she'd stay alive because he knew how to do his job. He knew how to keep her safe. He'd always keep her safe. What?

No. He'd just met her, even though it'd felt as if they'd been together for days. Months even. It hadn't been a day yet, and more so, he didn't— He couldn't—

He simply could not love her. Not that he did already. Heavens, he wasn't that flawed.

Falling in love—that he did not do. Not anymore. He had his work, his life, his family and friends. He was content not to have a needy female in his life to distract him from the things he needed to accomplish, and loving someone was always a distraction. He'd spent the past seven years guarding his heart and keeping his emotions in check. How much he enjoyed looking at her pretty face wasn't going to change that.

*Mr. Louden, while emotions dictate otherwise, need and want are not the same.*

He knew that well enough. He knew that quite well enough, because right now he could feel every lush curve, every warm contour. What he needed didn't match what he wanted in this moment. And he wanted—

"Malia," he said, his voice hoarse. As gently as he possibly could, Frank pushed her back, for his sake as much as hers. "Everything is going to be fine."

She was staring up at him. There was hope in her eyes, or at least a willingness to hope that all would end well. That she wanted to trust him was enough for him. For now.

He turned her around, to where she faced the entrance to the drawing room.

"Hello," he called out.

"Frank," Grandfather answered, "we're in here."

He nudged Miss Vaccarelli forward. They stepped into the drawing room.

"Oh, darling, it's so good to see—" Grandmother stopped halfway between them; her outstretched hands lowered. Her gaze shifted from Frank to Miss Vaccarelli then back to Frank. Something close to a smile flittered across her lips. It would not do, not do at all, for her to be rude and unwelcoming, but she didn't have to say a word or move a facial muscle. Her caution was evident.

Grandfather stood with his favorite Jules Verne novel, *From Earth to the Moon,* still in hand. Tipping his head toward Miss Vaccarelli, he walked to his wife. He then looked to Frank. "What brings you to Tuxedo?"

"It's complicated." Frank closed the distance between them, and didn't smile over how Miss Vaccarelli stayed right next to him. Nor did he wallow in the pleasure over her action. He kissed his grandmother's cheek, shook his grandfather's hand and made introductions.

"Have a seat." Grandfather motioned to the furniture.

Grandmother and Miss Vaccarelli sat on opposite ends of the sofa; Grandfather took the chair next to it. Frank glanced around for somewhere to sit. Whoever designed the drawing room must not have wanted people to sit and have a conversation, which was likely why he'd avoided this room until today. That and with all the paintings, who would want to sit where it felt like hundreds of eyes were staring down upon him, waiting to expose his sins.

He grabbed one of the chairs by the chess table and carried it over to the sofa. He placed it catty-corner to Miss Vaccarelli's side. His grandparents' return hadn't been in his plan, but he'd adapt.

He sat, saying, "This isn't a pleasure visit. Miss Malia Vaccarelli is a witness in a case, and I'd like to keep her here until the deposition hearing in three weeks."

Grandmother looked to Grandfather, but he was studying Miss Vaccarelli.

"Vaccarelli," he murmured. He stroked his Santa-bearded chin, pulling on the three-inch-long hairs at the tip. "Name sounds familiar."

"My maternal grandfather," Miss Vaccarelli said in a matter-of-fact voice, "is Gulian DeWitt. His youngest daughter, Marion, married my father, Carmine Vaccarelli. You probably read in the papers about the Vaccarelli yacht sinking off the New Jersey coast. Two years and three months ago. My parents and nonni all died in the explosion."

Frank's grandparents exchanged glances.

"We had read that," Grandfather admitted. "I know DeWitt. Good man."

Frank leaned forward, resting his elbows on his knees. "The mafiosi have put a hit out on Miss Vaccarelli's brother."

"Why?" asked Grandmother.

Frank paused. The truth was shameful enough without him having to embarrass Miss Vaccarelli in front of his grandparents.

"Giovanni is in the mafiosi, too," Miss Vaccarelli answered without hesitancy in her voice. Nor did her gaze lower to the ground. "I am trying to help him make more honorable choices. Your grandson has been a godsend, but I would not impose on your hospitality. Your safety is paramount to mine."

Grandmother's face paled. "Are we in danger?"

Grandfather reclaimed his book from the side table. Although his eyes narrowed as they did when he was analyzing a puzzle, he said nothing. A bear operator in the stock market, Charles Grahame didn't make his first—or fourth—million by letting others do the thinking and deciding for him.

"There's always a slight chance of danger," Frank admitted. "Only two other people know we are here, and they're both trusted marshals. I feel confident saying we're safe." For now.

Worth slid out from under the sofa, his cream-and-white fur standing on end from static electricity. He darted in a circle then barked once at Miss Vaccarelli.

"Sit," she said.

He didn't.

Still, she leaned down to pet him and—

"Don't," Frank blurted, grabbing her hand. "Watch." He moved his hand from hers to the dog and barely touched the fur when he felt the shock. Frank flinched. Worth yelped.

Grandfather snickered. "That hound conducts more electricity than Benjamin Franklin's kite."

Rising to the bait as she always did, Grandmother lifted her chin. "Worth is a direct descendant of Lenda and Marco from Queen Victoria's stock of Italian Volpinos and German spitzes. He is a blue blood. Not a hound. Not one of your retrievers. And he is still a puppy."

"Grandmother, you've been saying that for three years." Frank scratched behind the dog's ears. "You'd think he'd have learned by now that rolling under the sofa only makes it worse. For all his aristocratic heritage, this blond fellow is pretty worthless. He heeds no commands and has a penchant toward chewing socks."

"Now, Frank," Grandmother said and shifted her gaze to Miss Vaccarelli then back to him. Her thoughts practically screamed at him: *Good behavior in front of guests.*

Frank smiled at her. He knew how to win her over—a dip of his chin, lazy eyes, curved lips that said *I love you best, Grandmother.* As expected, the irritation in her eyes fled and she smiled back.

"One of my professors at Vassar," interjected Miss Vaccarelli, her gaze on Worth as she stroked his silky fur, "a man of dubious character and political associations, taught that the world was divided between the blonds, who had all the virtues, and the brunettes, who were decidedly inferior. He feared if something wasn't done about it, the fertile brunettes would overtake the virtuous blonds and make the world a very uncomfortable place." She looked up. "How can a dog this blond be deemed worthless? As a brunette myself, it pains me to admit he is a bastion against our oncoming apocalypse."

"Well, Frankie," Grandfather said, "the natural blonds that you, Worth and I are must band together against your grandmother and Miss Vaccarelli."

"It's a good thing we have them both in protective custody."

"The best place for them."

"You boys," Grandmother said with an amused sigh.

Miss Vaccarelli stopped petting Worth, but he nudged her into resuming. "Would he, by chance, be named after Charles Frederick Worth?"

Frank exchanged glances with his grandparents.

Grandmother shifted on the sofa to get a better look at her sofa mate. "You are the first to have guessed correctly. Everyone assumes he was named after Frank's older brother, Worthing."

Now there was a Louden who would never receive a lecture about not living up to potential. Neither would Worthing know how to laugh even if injected with a serum.

"My parents," Frank explained to Miss Vaccarelli, "went to England after their wedding. They—"

"Frank," warned Grandmother.

"—holidayed in Worthing," he said without pause. "My parents enjoy the ocean and fishing."

Miss Vaccarelli's lip, the side under that fascinating beauty mark, curved upward. "I take it they saw little of the beach."

"How right you are," Grandfather said quite proudly. Of Miss Vaccarelli's quip or his daughter and son-in-law's industriousness, Frank wasn't sure. He suspected both. Charles Grahame admired wit and dedication to duty.

Grandmother sent a glare his way, which Grandfather, per his nature, ignored.

Frank relaxed against the back of his chair, and Worth bounded uninvited into his lap. "If you would prefer we leave, we will."

A sigh ever so soft escaped Miss Vaccarelli's lips. It'd been a long day, but he knew she would never admit to being tired. Like a trouper, she would carry on until the battle ended.

Grandfather opened his book. "Leaving may be best."

Frank nodded. He didn't like his grandfather's decision, but he would respect it. Of course, the predicament now was where to hide Miss Vaccarelli. He needed somewhere safe, somewhere secluded and somewhere her reputation wouldn't be impugned. No sense worrying. An idea, he was confident, would come before they reached the Tuxedo front gate.

Frank nudged Worth off his lap. He stood. Miss Vaccarelli placed her hand in his, and he helped her to her feet. He let go as quickly as deemed proper, but his palm tingled from her touch. Something about her made him want to draw her close, shield her. Considering she was his first witness to protect, that made sense.

Grandfather grabbed his cane and moved to stand.

"Oh, Mr. Grahame," Miss Vaccarelli rushed out, "please don't stand on my account."

Yet he did.

"Meeting you has been my honor." She smiled at his grandparents. Her gaze moved around the room. "Your oil paintings are impressive, Mrs. Grahame. If I owned just half of them, I would turn one room of my home into a gallery and space each about the room so that I may take my leisure reading them. Every painting has a story, if you take the time to search for it."

Grandfather's eyes widened.

Grandmother gave her a strange look. "I had never thought of it that way. Sit, please, both of you."

Frank waited until Miss Vaccarelli found purchase on the sofa. He sat and stretched out his leg. What he wanted most at this moment was to remove the shoe encasing his splinted toe, but as long as the ladies were present, Frank, unlike his shoe-disliking grandfather, would remain shod.

"You may stay," Grandmother announced, "but we will need to give her a new name and a reason for being here."

Grandfather settled back in his chair. "How about... his fiancée?"

"No," blurted Miss Vaccarelli and Grandmother in unison.

"We can't pretend we're engaged," Frank explained with an apologetic shrug. "Certain things go with engagements. Tea parties, brunches, china patterns at Gimbels, announcement in the *Times,* etcetera, etcetera, etcetera." He leaned over the side of his chair and in a loud whisper said to Miss Vaccarelli, "Did I forget something, dearest person who refuses to be my faux fiancée?"

For someone he knew was peeved with his comment, she sat there with a placating smile. She had all the makings of the ideal wife.

Grandmother's foot tapped the carpet. "Frank, this is a serious matter."

"I'm a serious guy." He straightened in his seat, and Worth jumped on his lap again, and that's when he had the answer. "Miss Vaccarelli, how are you with static-y canines?"

Her mouth opened but nothing came out.

"I'll wager she can manage them," Grandfather put in, even though his attention was back on his book, "about as well as she can manage too-smart-for-their-own-good marshals."

Frank scooped up Worth and deposited him in her lap. "Sit."

He didn't.

"Congratulations, Miss Leah Carr," he announced under two confused gazes. "You are now the *governeresse*—or tutor, if you prefer—to a pompom with legs. Your duty is to watch over him morning, noon and night, and train him into good behavior. My grandfather thanks you for volunteering."

# Chapter 9

[T]here is always a happy combination of some attention on the part of the host and hostess, and the perfect freedom of the guests to occupy their time as they choose.

—Emily Price Post, *Etiquette*

*The next morning*
*10:23 a.m.*

With her arm outstretched from the dog's energetic pulling on the leash, Malia ordered, "Heel." Then, "Stop." Finally, "Whoa, doggie."

Worth, however, continued to pull. His nails clicked and scraped on the limestone steps in his desperation to reach the grass.

"I see improvement already," remarked Mr. Grahame.

Malia sighed in response. She descended the back steps,

in step with the reputable stockbroker. Top hat on head and cane in hand, he looked as if he were strolling along in Central Park, not that the air in the city ever tasted as fresh at that in the Ramapo Mountains. Between the puffy white clouds and the birds fluttering about the green tree-tops, even the sky looked bluer. Even with her heeled boots on, she was a head shorter than him.

"How do you like being a governess?" Mr. Grahame asked.

"Considering it is my first employment," Malia answered drily, "I have to say it suits me well. My charge woke me promptly at three o'clock for a morning constitutional."

"His bladder does favor the three o'clock hour."

She didn't have to look at him to know he was smiling. "After escorting me through the scenic path back to my room, he tutored me in the art of sharing by ensuring I stayed on one side of the bed."

"On the exact edge, I venture to guess."

"It is imperative one also learn the art of balancing."

Mr. Grahame thumped his cane on the last step. "I knew that hound was smarter than he let on," he said in that deep-chested voice of his.

Malia gave an approving nod. Contrary to Mr. Louden's repetitive insistence that the Pomeranian was worthless as he joined Malia on the tour the housekeeper had given her of the house—six bedrooms, over seven thousand square feet and a basement built into the bluff!—she'd developed fond feelings for Worth. After fourteen hours of nannying, he had the makings of her finest, albeit first and likely only, pupil. Not to say she didn't need a bit of tutoring on the difference between Pomeranians and Spitzes. Mr. Louden had simplified: Pomeranian was to Spitz as zucchini was to squash.

They stepped off the stairs and stopped where the pala-

tial limestone and hewn native stone ended and the manicured lawn, or at least the small patch there was on the
hillside, began. Worth ran in circles at the toes of Malia's
white lace-up boots that few could see under her borrowed
black cambric dress and high-bib apron. She could have
accepted a new pair of shoes, but like those silver slippers
Dorothy put on, these fit her fine. Besides, she liked having something daily to remind her of who she really was:
Malia Vaccarelli, heiress, not Leah Carr, dog governess.

"Then," she continued, "over breakfast, Worth kindly
spared me from kippers that were sure to upset my stomach."

Mr. Grahame's lips twitched. "You don't say."

"Your chef even complimented him with a fluttering of
adjectives best suited to anyone illiterate in French." Despite the chef's abhorrence for the dog, like the other eight
members of the staff, he had been most welcoming to her.
The Pomeranian, they'd all declared, needed expert training. She needed training if she wanted to have any hope
she could help him.

Mr. Grahame thumped his cane on the next step. "I had
no idea my wife's Pomeranian had such fine manners."

"Nor does he," Malia said with a sad sigh.

Mr. Grahame laughed.

"Sit," Malia ordered, pointing at the dog.

Worth, the industrious dog he was, stood on his back
paws, his front ones on her knee.

"At least he performed something on command." Malia
unclipped Worth's leash. "Go on. Attend to your business,"
she said, sliding the leash into her apron pocket.

Mr. Grahame rested his cane over his arm. Malia
watched him for a moment, waiting for him to confess his
reason for asking if he could join her on the walk. When
he said nothing, she followed his gaze to the dog dashing
around rough-hewn rocks in search of the best tree. The

silence lingered. Malia didn't mind, nor did Mr. Grahame seem bothered.

From what she'd seen since arriving, he was beloved by his wife and his staff, who praised him to Malia behind his back. From the glances she'd caught him giving his wife over dinner, she suspected Mrs. Grahame was as beloved. He was also an avid reader, which she'd guessed by the book he carried in the pocket of his tailored morning coat. The book's cover was gray, thus not *The Wonderful Wizard of Oz,* which she was yearning to finish. He seemed a deep and intellectual man, so she suspected his book was something deep and intellectual as well, such as the writings of Plato or Saint Augustine.

He cleared his throat. "You are the first girl Frank has brought to visit since his divorce."

Malia blinked, startled by his abrupt announcement. She turned her head enough to look directly at him and opened her mouth to respond, but his gaze was on the dog, which was still looking for that prime watering hole. Not any spot would do, as she'd learned at three in the morning.

"I can't imagine his life has been easy since his wife left him."

"No, it hasn't. I know you're in protective custody," he went on. "Frank seems...different here."

"He is here for work, sir, not pleasure. I'm sure he is focusing on doing his job."

He shook his head. "That's not what I mean." His blue eyes settled on her. "He seems different here *with you.*"

Malia nodded even though she wasn't sure what to make of his comment. Mr. Louden behaved the same with her as he'd had with Miss Hogan, and as he had when he'd spoken to the housekeeper and even with his grandmother. Was this "different" a good thing? Or bad? She was about to ask when Worth came running up. He sat at Malia's feet and scratched frantically at his neck, growling, as he had several times since she'd become his caretaker.

"Is this normal?" she asked.

"You're the dog governess."

"Because your grandson volunteered me!" she said, chuckling. She then drew in a deep breath. "Mr. Grahame, I should have confessed this last night. Never in my life have I owned a pet. The closest I come to dogs are when I'm walking in Central Park. I know nothing about them."

"Excellent. This means I can reduce your salary."

She stared, mind blank at how to respond to a man whose humor was so much like his grandson's. Splendid. Because she couldn't quite argue about her salary when they both knew full well she wasn't receiving one, she knelt next to Worth. She was the dog's governess, so, by golly, she would be the best one there ever was. As Worth's white fox face stared up at her, she pressed her fingers through the fur in search of bumps, lesions or splinters. Found none. Whatever was bothering him wasn't on his skin.

He twisted his neck and continued to growl, this time using a front paw to push at his two-inch-wide jeweled collar.

Malia scooped him in her arms and stood. "Sir, the problem is his collar and, more precisely, his lack of love for it."

Mr. Grahame stepped closer. He examined the dog. Before Malia could blink, he bent the collar. The clasp snapped. Worth began licking Malia's hands, his sandpapery tongue determined not to miss a spot.

*"Instead of the cross, the Albatross about my neck was hung."* Mr. Grahame pocketed the collar. "Now there. That will give you and Worth some peace until Josie has it repaired."

"You knew?" Malia placed the dog on the ground. He immediately darted to the steps.

"No male—human or canine—wants to wear a jewelry store about his neck." Mr. Grahame gave her an apologetic look. "My wife bought the collar in Paris last week, and Worth has been scratching ever since."

Malia joined him in walking back to the stairs. She lifted the hem of her skirt as she ascended in the middle, leaving the handrail for Mr. Grahame. Save for his knees, the man seemed in excellent health for someone his age.

"Why haven't you told her Worth dislikes it?" she asked.

"For the same reason I haven't told her the problem with her drawing room. Every designer has had to work under the stipulation he include *all* the paintings and tapestries in the design. Josie doesn't like to be told what to do." He gave her a sidelong glance. "But you graciously put the solution in her mind, and for that I am in your debt."

They reached the curve onto the second-floor balcony. Down below was the carriage house, paved drive and Mr. Louden washing Miss Hogan's vehicle. The brown coat of the three-piece suit he'd borrowed from his grandfather lay across an iron bench. His shirtsleeves rolled above his elbows, revealing the toned muscles of his forearms and what was either a birthmark or a tattoo. The latter wouldn't surprise her. King Edward VII's tattoos made them popular among High Society. One didn't need more than a day's acquaintance to know that Frank Louden was comfortable in his own skin, flaws and all.

She admired that in him. She envied that.

Feeling his grandfather's eyes upon her, Malia turned around to appreciate, instead, the expansive stretch of shimmering blue water called Tuxedo Lake that was no less enchanting in the day as it had been under the moonlight at three o'clock in the morning.

Mr. Grahame leaned back against the side wall. "I take it you like what you see."

Malia couldn't help but nod. She liked everything she could see—and had seen—although she hoped he wasn't referring to his grandson. Still, her cheeks warmed. On the far left, above the treetops, she caught a glimpse of a partially built cottage (mansion, really) on the hill next to the one the Grahame estate was perched majestically on, the sounds of the construction faint in the distance. The main view, though, was of the virginal mountains rising on the far shore of the lake.

"There is a serenity here not found in the city," she admitted.

"A man can find his soul in these mountains. Or lose it. I've done both."

She leaned back, resting her palms on the limestone wall cap, the stone cold and rough against her skin. Yet unlike anything she experienced in the city, this felt real. This felt alive, and inviting to new birth.

*"And though I have the gift of prophecy,"* she said softly, *"and understand all mysteries, and all knowledge; and though I have all faith, so that I could remove mountains, and have not love, I am nothing."*

That seemed to surprise him. "You are more than I expected, Governess."

She gave him an easy smile. This man was in the upper echelon of Society, and, according to the chambermaid, owned a cottage in Tuxedo, a mansion on Millionaire's Row and a beach house in Newport, and he traveled to Paris once a year. He was less than she'd expected, and in that she was glad to be wrong.

"I envy your view," she admitted. "If I were to live anywhere besides New York, it would be near green mountains and water, and where the air smells of earth and rain."

"DeWitt would want to know where you are."

It was his turn to surprise her. "Grandfather hasn't spoken to me since the funeral. My family brings shame upon him, and—" She took in an unexpected breath. A wave of anguish pounded into her chest. "And...as much as I would wish—" Her voice caught. Splendid. She was going to cry. Again. This was not her, a person who wept at the first tug on the heartstring. A cornucopia of tears.

She turned swiftly, looked over her shoulder, blinking rapidly to dry her eyes.

After Mamma died, Grandfather DeWitt was free to end any duty he had to them. No more visits because Mamma invited—begged—him to come. No more pretending he didn't despise Malia and Giovanni for being the offspring of a disobedient union. No more being anything in her life. For all that he wasn't anymore, she still missed him.

Alone. That's what she was. That's all she'd ever be. She had no life within the mafiosi. How could she have any life outside it?

"Are you going to tell Grandfather DeWitt where I am?"

"It's not my place, Malia." Mr. Grahame's hand covered hers. "Burying a loved one is as hard for a parent as it is for a child." After a gentle squeeze, he walked away.

Malia looked to the sky, expecting to see clouds, dark and gloomy. But the sky was bright. The sky showed no fear. The sky carried no burdens. The sky was light and free and unchained. Any shadows there were had settled on her heart. Were they holding her, or, God help her, was she clinging to them? All coppers *weren't* corrupt. She could see that now. Had she been poisoned, too, about her grandfather?

He wasn't going to look at her. Not again.

Frank focused on drying—in a clockwise motion and with an Egyptian cotton towel—the leather bench. Whatever Miss Vaccarelli and Grandfather were discussing was between them. What she did with her time was her business. Hers. Not his. They had no relationship. None. They could have no relationship.

"None," he muttered, keeping his back turned to the balcony. He moved to the backseat and dried it.

"Darling, I don't see why you couldn't have left that to the sunshine."

Frank looked up to see his grandmother approaching with a crystal goblet of lemonade, her olive-green mermaid skirt sweeping the ground. She stopped next to him, kissed his cheek and gave him the glass.

Frank took a long sip. "How was Paris?"

"As expected," she simply said. "I am not pleased you brought her here."

Frank couldn't stop himself from glancing up to the second-story staircase, where Miss Vaccarelli no longer was. She had to have Worth with her, and the dog wasn't allowed access to the upper floors except his grandparents' bedroom and, now, hers, out of fear of what he'd eat or use as a chew bone. It wasn't as if she had many things to do throughout the day, so she probably needed help—

No, he wasn't going to investigate. Or wonder. What she did with her time wasn't his business. And he would cease thinking about her, even though she hadn't left his mind since he saw her in the hotel courtyard. The prettiest flower there.

He looked back at his grandmother. "Since you feel that way, why did you tell us to stay?"

Her head tilted as she looked at him. "I did so because she is a charming young woman whom you find quite attractive."

Frank drank until the glass was empty, and his mouth, at least, felt refreshed. He could argue that her comment—and accusation—wasn't true, but considering it was, he saw little point. He gave her the empty glass, which she took and held with both hands.

"Thank you," he said.

"Hmmph."

"What is that supposed to mean?"

"You know."

He stared at her as if she'd lost her mind. He now understood why his grandfather said it was pointless to argue with a woman because women expect men to understand what they were unable to communicate. Any other conversation, he'd let it go. But this had something to do with Miss Vaccarelli, and he couldn't let that go. She was a witness. His responsibility.

"If I were a woman," he began slowly, "I would know what you mean because those of your kind speak in grunts, sighs, single syllables and facial expressions that you all inherently understand." He laid the damp towel across the floorboard for the sunlight to dry it. "Grandmother, I love you—you know I do—but I'm a thirty-year-old man who needs a translation."

She regarded him coolly. "She is not in your class."

Frank rubbed at the growing tension between his brows. Somehow what she was saying made sense, at least, to her. "Thank God she isn't a pariah because her spouse left her for someone else."

"You aren't a pariah."

Frank saw little point in responding.

"James and Cora Brown Potter divorced last year."

Their divorce, and Cora's affairs, didn't make him feel any less shame over his divorce or Rose's amorous intrigues. Society's code, established by H.R.H, the Prince of Wales, permitted seeking a soul mate outside the boundaries of marriage. After all, Americans had the right, as Rose had claimed upon informing she was seeking a divorce, to "the pursuit of happiness;" therefore, she was not "obligated to be yoked for life to an incompatible husband."

Grandmother didn't look any more pleased to add, "Rumor has it the Tailer-Lorillard marriage is ending too."

"Why are you telling me this?"

"Because you like her," she said even though that had already been established.

"I like pie," he snapped, "and you aren't lecturing me over that."

"I don't mind if you have pie. I do mind—" Her eyes narrowed, her voice lowered. "Frank, you can be a real pill when you want to be."

"Thank you."

She leveled a flat stare in his direction.

"I'm sorry," he rushed out. "I thought you were complimenting me." He gave her a smile, the one that always won her over.

This time she looked away. Her lips pursed, and he knew it wasn't in an attempt to hide a grin. When she looked back, her light eyes brimmed with tears. She patted them dry with the tips of her fingers just as Malia had in Cady's office.

She released a breath. "Once Miss Vacca— Once *she* testifies at the deposition hearing," she said firmly, "you will never see her again."

"Don't you think I know that?" Frank gritted his teeth.

Malia appealed to him, and on too many levels, yet knowledge of what lay before her twenty days from now was ever present in his mind. She had no future in New York. None. Malia Vaccarelli had to die to this life, for her own safety. He was a deputy marshal for the United States, on his way to rise to his full potential and become chief marshal of the Southern District of New York. There was no possible way he could have a future with her, even if he wanted one. Attraction did not equate to marriage.

Frank gave his grandmother a hug. "I appreciate your concern." He held her until he could feel her relax. Her violet-and-vanilla perfume took him back to his childhood and youth when she initiated the hugs after he'd been punished for something that didn't bring honor to the family. "Save your worry for a more worrisome cause." He drew back. "Please."

She looked at him as if she wasn't convinced, yet she said, "I trust you to do what is best."

That struck him as odd.

Why *best?* Why not *right* or *wise?* He'd ask, but, really, could a man ever understand a woman's reasoning?

As she walked back inside the house, Frank checked his pocket watch. He had enough time to grab a bite to eat and warn Miss Vaccarelli that the police were coming.

# *Chapter 10*

If you know one who is gay, beguiling and amusing, you will, if you are wise, do everything you can to make him prefer your house and your table to any other; for where he is, the successful party is also.
—Emily Price Post, *Etiquette*

*Grahame Receiving Room*
*An hour or so later*

Mrs. Grahame on her right, Malia sat in the middle of the quite firm sofa. Per the dictates of the etiquette books she'd studied tirelessly during her teen years in hopes of learning correct Society speech and behavior, she sat straight-backed, shoulders level and hands clasped demurely in her lap to hide her nervousness. Worth lay on the ground at Mrs. Grahame's feet, snoring to his contentment.

On the matching red sofa across from them sat Gillmore

"Gil" Bush, Tuxedo Park police captain, and Charlie Patterson, park superintendent. From the moment Mr. Louden and his grandfather were called from the room by the butler, the captain and superintendent spoke to Mrs. Grahame and looked everywhere except at Malia. She hoped that was because they didn't want to make her feel like a zoo animal on display. They could be trusted, though, or so Mr. Louden and his grandfather had said. Since she trusted—

She schooled the smile that wanted to grow. She trusted Mr. Louden. She felt safe here with him and his family. The Grahames were a true godsend.

"No, ma'am," Superintendent Patterson was saying to Mrs. Grahame. "With the Orange Turnpike the only real means of escape, even professional burglars have shunned Tuxedo."

"It's too easy to get lost in the woods and hills," Captain Bush explained before Malia or Mrs. Grahame could question why.

Mr. Patterson eased forward, clearly excited to elaborate. "In one rare instance, a perpetrator wasn't caught on the turnpike. We apprehended him in the woods two days later. He was lost, half-starved, and still had the loot on him. There's no safer place in New York than Tuxedo."

Mrs. Grahame patted Malia's clenched hands. "See, you have nothing to fear."

She wanted to believe.

She had no reason not to believe.

Right now she would feel better if Mr. Louden would return and tell her all was well. Malia looked longingly to the empty front foyer. What was so pressing they had to discuss it now?

"Frankie, my boy, you have a problem," Grandfather said, cutting into the silence that had lingered for several minutes, giving them time to make sense of the literal news the butler had called them out of the parlor to impart.

Indeed, this was unexpected.

As they sat on the marble staircase next to each other, Frank stared at the announcement in the Wednesday edition of the *Times*.

> *Mr. Edwin Craig Daly*
> *Miss Malia DeWitt Vaccarelli*
> *Engaged At Home*
> *Sunday, April 7, 1901*
> *826 Fifth Avenue*

It wasn't a real announcement. The Malia Vaccarelli he knew would never willingly agree to marry the conniving assistant D.A. She certainly wouldn't have spent Easter Sunday with him, at his bachelor residence, unless a chaperone was present, which Malia had to have insisted upon in addition to her brother. Daly's parents would have been there too. What was he thinking? The announcement wasn't real. She was never in Daly's home.

Frank crumpled the newsprint. Jealousy made his mouth sour. He could never have a future with her himself, but until this moment, he didn't realize how deeply he wished things were different.

"This isn't a problem," he said, forcing pragmatism into his thoughts. "This tells us something."

Grandfather's brows rose. "What is that?"

"When an engagement is made between two socially prominent people, reporters are sent to get further information," he said, and his grandfather began nodding as if was catching on to Frank's reasoning. "Details, such as entertainments to be given or wedding plans, will be asked for." Frank paused. He waited until his grandfather's gaze leveled with his.

He then added, "What does every reporter desire the most?

"A photograph of the happy couple."

"More specifically…a photograph of the future bride."

Grandfather spoke with quiet amazement. "When Daly can't produce a photograph of Miss Vaccarelli, the reporters will go in search of one. It'll be a contest to see who can print one first."

"Hopefully it'll take time to find a photo."

"Could be days."

"Could be weeks," Frank offered, trying to be hopeful.

"Once one society page has a photo, all the dailies will follow suit."

"And still it could be days, weeks even, before someone connects Leah Carr, dog governess, with Malia Vaccarelli. Time is still on our side." Frank took a deep breath and let it out slowly, the exhale whiffling away his tension. "Daly needs that picture because his bosses need it. The mafiosi can't find her if they don't know what she looks like."

Grandfather grinned. "If they don't know what she looks like, it's even more unlikely they know she's here."

Malia breathed a sigh of relief the moment Messrs. Louden and Grahame reentered the parlor looking rather smug—yet so utterly alike—in their three-piece suits. Were it not for forty-six years between them and Mr. Grahame's white beard, they could be brothers. Even their walk, with the slight hitch to the left leg, was the same. Mr. Grahame returned to the chair he had vacated in the bottom of the U-shaped furniture arrangement facing the hand-carved stone, floor-to-ceiling fireplace. He stretched his arm out, and his wife grabbed his hand.

Instead of returning to his chair next to his grandfather, Mr. Louden took the empty seat on the sofa next to Malia. He sat back, crossing his right ankle over his left knee; thus, his thigh pressed against hers. "Thank you for waiting on me."

"Is anything wrong?" inquired Mrs. Grahame.

Mr. Louden shook his head. "The mafiosi are desperate to find Miss Vaccarelli. We believe they don't have a photograph of her but are now in the pursuit of one. Once an image hits the dailies, the risk of someone here recognizing her increases." He leaned forward and rested his elbows on his knees, focusing on the men on the sofa opposite them. "How much access do the immigrant laborers have to the park?"

"Before they can enter the gate," Superintendent Patterson answered, "they must show a numbered work permit, which gives them access to the park during the day. They are only allowed to use the side roads—the main Tuxedo Road being reserved for gentlemen and ladies."

"With our police crew patrolling the park day and night," Mr. Bush put in, "it is unlikely any of the workers will trespass onto Grahame land. I do advise Miss Vaccarelli to stay inside when any deliveries are made to the house."

"I shall send word rescheduling tea and bridge," Mrs. Grahame announced.

"No," blurted Messers. Louden, Grahame, Patterson and Bush.

Mr. Grahame looked to his wife. "Josie, we need to maintain a semblance of normality. When any of our friends visit, Frank will ensure Miss Vaccarelli stays out of sight."

Mr. Louden shifted on the sofa, his knee bumping against hers. "Look at the captain and superintendent."

She did as he asked. The two men couldn't be more opposite. In his navy blue police uniform similar to what the Metropolitans wore, Mr. Bush was a fine figure of a man, over six feet tall with broad shoulders and an important-looking mustache. Mr. Patterson, in his dress blues—the shade closer to Egyptian blue than navy—was a stocky, sandy-haired, energetic man, who'd all but glowed when he'd spoken of park security. Both seemed genuinely sincere about keeping her safe.

"You know art." Mr. Louden leaned close, his shoulder against hers, his head tilted slightly toward her ear. "You have an artist's eyes. Study their uniforms. The hat…" he said softly, and she could hear the roughness in his voice, feel the warmth of his breath, smell his cedar-and-spice cologne.

He was saying something more, but she wasn't listening. Couldn't hear anything over her heartbeat. She felt fluttery, and warm, and if she turned her head—and it would be so easy to—their lips would touch. The first time she desired to kiss a man, and, how ironic, it had to be the man charged by the courts to guard her. An honorable man. A good man. A man she could trust not to hide the truth—good or bad—from her. She could love a man like him.

She gave her head a little shake. She was being fanciful. Details. Pay attention to the details. To his voice.

"…and the color of the cloth," he was saying. "The texture and weave. The number of buttons. Is there any difference between the badge on the hat and on the lapel? If so, find it."

She kept her eyes on the men yet turned her face a fraction, and whispered, "Why do I have to know this?"

"When you know the original, you won't be deceived by the forgery."

Malia swallowed. This was a test, and he believed she had enough of an eye for detail to spot a fraud. He believed she could do it. He believed in her.

He handed her his badge, then relaxed back against the sofa, his right foot crossed again over the left knee. Messrs. Patterson and Bush gave her their badges to study also.

Once she'd finished, the Grahames walked with the men to the door.

"Malia?"

She looked to Mr. Louden, his arm stretched across the sofa back and armrest. Someday it would be nice to scoot back on the sofa and curl up next to a man. They'd sit by the fire, and talk, and read, and enjoy just being together. She could do it now. She wanted to even though she knew it wasn't proper and knew his grandparents could walk in and see them.

Leah Carr would do it. Leah Carr was brave and adventurous.

But Leah Carr wasn't her. New clothes and a new identity didn't change the fact she was Malia Vaccarelli, daughter of and sister to the mafiosi.

His lips moved into a wry hint of a smile. "The dailies all posted engagement announcements between you and Edwin Daly." She must have looked mortified because he said, "I know it's not real. The mafiosi are desperate to find you."

She nodded. Really, there wasn't much to say in response.

"The estate is protected from view by heavy trees and rocky terrain." He checked his watch then returned it to the pocket in his waistcoat. "I've made a decision."

She waited. He sounded so final...and foreboding... and serious.

"You can take Worth out when he needs to go," he continued. "For your safety, I'm not letting you out of my sight."

She blinked, stunned. "At all?"

"Obviously during sleeping hours, and when you need to, uh...attend to, uh..." His cheeks reddened. "Other than that, at all hours, unless I need to leave you in Grandfather's care. I'll set an alarm to wake me up at three o'clock, so you don't have to take Worth out alone."

She continued to stare.

"You can be the dog governess, and I'll be the witness nanny, if that's all right with you?"

He quirked a brow. Grinned. Gave her a look that made her legs feel rather liquid, and she needed to sit down. Only she was. Sitting, that is. And she knew now why Irene had warned her not to look at him when he grinned; she knew why. At the first bloom of his devastating smile, she'd begun nodding in complete agreement as if he was giving her the world.

And this man was insisting on not letting her out of his sight.

Splendid.

*Day eight of twenty-one*
*2:42 p.m.*

Two coffee mugs in hand, Frank stepped into the library. Malia stood at the top of the three-step library ladder attached to a railing on the cabinet. Clad in her strangely alluring maid's getup, she stretched to reach a book on the upper shelf, left foot perched precariously on a step, while her other leg provided balance. Worth sat in the corner at the feet of the parlor maid, who should have been the one procuring the book but was knitting instead.

He wasn't surprised.

Malia Vaccarelli did not expect others to serve her when the deed was something she could do herself. She truly was the kindhearted soul Anne Morgan had described her as, beautiful inside and out. When he questioned the staff, they all praised her effortlessly...with one exception. Her dog-training skills were lacking, but, of course, they all blamed Worth for being "probably unteachable."

There was no "probably" about it.

Grandfather finally looked up from his book. "Ah,

Frankie, glad you're back." To Frank's chagrin, he dog-eared the page he was reading. "What did Dr. Rushmore say about your broken toe?"

Frank walked to the two oversize chairs seated behind an octagonal table and set on each side of the unlit fireplace. For all the masculinity of the room—mahogany wood, evergreen papered walls, animal-skin rugs—his grandmother had chosen to center a crystal chandelier above the table, as if to remind the room's inhabitants that the library wasn't for men only.

The bright sky and warm weather called to him. But since he had to keep Malia inside until the ladies who were there for Grandmother's tea departed, the cathedral-ceiling library in the Queen Anne tower was his favorite place to be. After his divorce, he'd spent many hours on that window seat under the leaded-glass windows, staring out at the lake.

Windows didn't condemn.

He handed his grandfather a mug, then turned to Malia to see how she would react to his spurious announcement. "Rushmore mentioned amputation."

Her lips twitched, yet she continued to focus on loosening the book.

"You don't say," Grandfather mused.

Frank settled in the other seat, which gave him a prime view of his favorite witness. He was feeling too jaunty to not say, "In the end, instead of removing the splint, he suggested waiting another week to see if the gangrene goes away. I could die. But he gave me four-to-three odds."

Grandfather's brows rose. "Of living or dying?"

"In my elation to have such favorable odds, I rather forgot to ask." Frank felt his head tilt as he watched Malia, now standing on the tiptoes of her left foot, although with her right hand, she wisely clenched a shelf. "Do you think what you are doing is safe?"

Her fingertips pinched at the book. "Your grandfather said it was."

Frank looked to his grandfather.

"I may have said that."

"May?"

Grandfather drank his coffee. His beard hid any possible grin.

Malia grunted, drawing Frank's attention again. Her nails scraped at the book's spine, yet it didn't ease free of its close-knit neighbors. "Almost...got...it."

"You could ask for help," Frank offered before sipping his coffee. He'd move to help her, but the library chair was a leather-covered cloud, and she appeared to have it under control. "Or you could move the ladder, since you are quite determined to do this yourself."

"Yes," she said gravely, "I could."

Frank drank his coffee and waited for her to say more. She didn't.

Grandfather placed his mug on the table. "She has a point there."

"How is that a point?" Frank asked.

Neither his grandfather nor Malia proposed an answer.

"Sir, pardon me," the parlor maid said in a low voice. "Worth is licking my hands. Does this mean something?"

Grandfather looked to Malia. "Well, Governess?"

She released a loud sigh. "I've decided it is his means of communicating his desire to go outside. Let me get this book, Ernestina, and then I'll take him." Her fingertips continued to scrape against the spine.

"He could want a drink," Frank supplied. "Or one of Grandfather's socks."

Grandfather gave him a look, the one that said *don't argue with the governess.*

"I should take him." The parlor maid scooped the dog up into her arms. "Madam's guests won't notice me."

Grandfather put down his book, claimed his mug then grabbed his cane, standing. "I'll walk with you. Josie is sure to be serving cake, and her lady friends are sure to not be eating any." He stepped around the table. "I'll return shortly. With cake."

Frank stared at him. This was the same man who had complained over breakfast of the aching in his knee. "You can have food brought to you."

"Yes. I could," he said in the same monotone Malia had used. He continued to the opened door, a step in front of the parlor maid. "Don't let her fall."

Frank looked from the departing back of his grandfather to Malia shooting ocular daggers at the wedged book. He put his mug down then walked over. "What's this book you're so desperate for?"

"It's called *Practical Dog Training*."

A chuckle burst forth. "Grandfather has pulled the wool over you. There isn't a book in this room with that title." If there were one, Frank would know because...well, he'd know.

After another scrape of her nails failed to gain purchase of the book, she straightened on the ladder. She grabbed the shelf with both hands and rested her forehead against it, sighing. "I should have just moved the ladder."

He raised his hands in the air. "Why didn't I think of that?"

"Yes, why didn't you?" With a droll sideways glance, she started down a step.

"Wait," he rushed out. "Allow me to be of assistance." He placed his hands on her waist. "I'll steady you, and you grab the Book That Doesn't Actually Exist."

For the longest moment, he didn't think she was going to move. He didn't mind. With her tobacco-brown hair piled atop her head, nothing obscured the smooth line of her neck or the soft golden tone to her skin. After a week of shared meals, dog walks, chess and domino matches, and lots of conversations during, after, and in between, he knew her political and religious leanings (same as his), favorite books (not the same as his) and worst childhood experience involving a sibling and scissors (could have been the same if his mother hadn't rescued him).

His fascination with her had only been compounded upon discovering that Malia Vaccarelli had a sense of humor and wicked competitive streak. The woman had to be his twin. Shadow. Match.

*A loss,* she'd repeatedly said, *is only one attempt closer to a win.* And that had been her means of consoling him. Him!

Frank grinned, even though she wasn't looking at him. Even more so because she wasn't looking at him. If he managed it right—and he knew how to manage it right— with a little shift in his hold, she would be in his arms. He could do it. He wanted to do it.

His fingers flinched, and that jolted her.

Malia leaned to the side, putting her weight literally in his hands. She snatched the book off the shelf then settled, feet flat, onto the ladder step before dropping down to the bottom step, at eye level. "Voilà." She held the book before her rising and falling chest, the blue cover facing forward.

Sure enough, in white embossed lettering were the words—

*Practical Dog Training:*
*Or, Training Vs.*
*Breaking*

*Stephen Tillinghast Hammond*

He met her gaze. "Is this where you gloat?"
Her brows raised a fraction, chin dipped. "Frank

Louden, I would have you know," she lectured in a stern voice that reminded him of his sisters' old governess, "gloating is, um—" Her lips pinched, trembled. Her face reddened, and he wasn't too sure she was breathing. She burst out laughing. A lovely, throaty sound, it was elegant yet unrestrained to the proper mores of Society. Nothing could capture her spirit more.

Frank did the only logical thing a situation like this dictated. He moved close. He placed his shoe on the lower step, against hers, and gripped the ladder frame so that in no way could she descend without tripping over him. Unless she was, say, a kangaroo. Or a frog.

He leaned forward a touch. "I believe you're laughing at me."

She moistened her lips, schooled her smile, amusement gone. Then her brows rose dubiously. "Is that so?" She glanced around. "Peculiar that you say so, for I hear no laughter."

"Now who's too smart for her own good?"

A little hmmph. A little shrug. Then her lashes lowered over her eyes, lips curved mischievously. She met his gaze and—

The ladder, the books, the walls floated away, and all there was, was him and her and this moment. Frank stopped breathing. He wanted to kiss her. He needed to kiss her. From the way she was looking at him, he knew she wanted it too. She wouldn't instigate it; she was too proper to do anything so bold. Yet her lips parted. A little sigh escaped on her sweet breath. All he had to do was lean forward and draw her achingly close to him. One kiss. One. One touch of his lips to her pink, moist and not particularly unique ones until her Creator, like a master artiste, had added the dot above her lip. Ordinary into extraordinary. But one kiss wouldn't be enough. It would never be enough.

A kiss wasn't his to have. If he did kiss her, he wouldn't be able to let her go. He was a marshal. She was a witness. She had to leave New York and start a new life, which meant he had to do the best thing for both of them, even if it meant dying to all he'd wanted. There wasn't anything more he wanted in this moment than her.

*Jesus, I am weak. Be strong in me.*

Frank stepped back. He assisted her to the floor. "Why the book?" he said and found solace in the superficiality of the question.

Malia nipped at her bottom lip. She turned from Mr. Louden and walked to the chairs by the table. He'd almost kissed her. Her heart was still flittering about from the way he'd been looking at her mouth. And she'd done nothing but stand there in hopeful anticipation, practically begging for him to kiss her. Which he didn't because he wasn't weak as she was. Splendid. How embarrassing.

With a sigh, she sat in the chair that Mr. Grahame had vacated. Her mind sought what it was that Mr. Louden had asked her, and her gaze fell to the book she clenched to her chest.

Mr. Louden reclaimed his seat and his coffee.

"Your grandmother adores Worth." She silently cheered that her voice sounded normal. "In gratitude to her, I feel I should at least attempt to teach him proper etiquette, even if it is only to sit upon command. I went to your grandfather for advice, and he said he'd look into finding me a book."

He relaxed against the back of his chair, his left leg stretched out before him. "He did train his hunting dogs." Instead of looking at her, he stared absently at the window across from them. He seemed distracted, maybe a bit unsure. And from what she knew of Frank Louden, he wasn't a man to wallow in self-doubt.

Since he said no more, Malia opened the book and forced her mind to focus on the words.

The minutes passed slowly. With each turn of the page, her pulse returned to normal, and she forgot about what could have happened and the awkward aftermath. Mr. Louden found a book to read too.

Eventually Mr. Grahame returned with Ernestina and Worth, and without any cake. Malia insisted he take the nicer chair. After settling on the window seat, and in the warm rays of the sun, she resumed reading. The occasional turning of a page was the only sound in the room. Her pupil was a bit older than the puppy age recommended best for training, but for the first time since being volunteered to be his "governess," she felt more equipped for the task.

Minutes passed in companionable silence.

"Oh, Mr. Louden, listen to this." Malia held the book to chin level. "*You should also speak to him using intelligent, rational language, such as you would use in talking to a ten-year-old boy, and you will be surprised at how soon he will understand your conversation.* Why ten? Why not nine or eleven or fifteen? Shouldn't one talk to a dog as one does to any age boy? Or a man for that matter?"

She turned to him. His eyes were closed, head resting against the back of the chair, open book flat on his chest. She could imagine him just like that except with a wheat-blond child asleep on his lap. His wife would replace the book with a blanket and then caress the child's cheek before leaving a kiss on his. Her heart ached.

"Are you asleep?" she asked.

An easy grin returned to Mr. Louden's face. "Woof. Woof, woof."

## Chapter 11

> [The perfect guest] has merely acquired a habit, born
> of many years of arduous practise, of turning every-
> thing that looks like a dark cloud as quickly as pos-
> sible for the glimmer of a silver lining.
> —Emily Price Post, *Etiquette*

*Day fifteen of twenty-one*
*9:16 a.m.*

Malia's fingers nipped at the bits of jerky and crackers
in her apron pocket as she stood just inside the entrance
to the French drawing room. A week's worth of study and
training prepared her for adding a second pupil. "Madam,
before we begin, it is imperative you understand that Worth
is cunning and obstinate."

Mrs. Grahame in a teal day dress sat with her back
turned to her desk. She said nothing, nor did her stately

expression communicate any emotion except unabashed interest in what Malia had to say next.

Mr. Louden, sitting in a chair next to her, though, leaned against his grandmother's shoulder. In a loud whispered voice, he said, "You're paying her *how much* to tell you something everyone in this house already knows?"

She shushed him. "Go on, Miss Carr."

Malia dipped her head. "Thank you, madam. Being that he is cunning and obstinate, Worth will persistently refuse to obey, which is why it is imperative that you exercise firmness, patience and kindness."

She glanced down at Worth, who still sat as she'd commanded him. After seven days of lessons, he had one trick down.

"Good sit," she said sweetly and gave him a treat. She looked to her human pupil. "Dogs do not by instinct understand the English language."

Mr. Louden held a hand up. "How about French? Grandmother knows French."

For all his sassy looks, alluring cedar cologne and fine-tailored suit, Malia ignored him. "A dog obeys a certain command given by a particular person because he has learned that sounds uttered are to be followed by some act of his own. When a dog loves his master, his greatest pleasure will be the sense that he is pleasing you." She looked to Worth, sweetly repeated, "Good sit," and then gave him another jerky.

"Is it necessary I carry treats on me?" Mrs. Grahame inquired.

Mr. Louden opened his mouth, and Malia cut him off with a look.

"No, madam," she answered. "While you are training Worth, be unstinting with your praise. When he has behaved creditably, your adulation will be his chief reward." She paused. She needed to be serious. Indeed, she did.

This was, after all, a serious moment of instruction for Mrs. Grahame's benefit. But a minute in Frank's presence brought out her cheekiness.

She kept her voice level. "Although, common to those of the male sex, a bit of some food he likes should often accompany the kind words, and you will win his devotion."

Mr. Louden's smile turned positively serene. "I'm in love."

Mrs. Grahame gave him a look, one Malia didn't find hard to interpret: *Oh, Frank, hush.*

"Lessons," Malia continued, "should be given two to three times a day, and should be short. Madam, if you would please approach—"

"Frank!" Mr. Grahame's deep-chested voice came from the foyer behind her.

Malia looked over her shoulder as he strode into the drawing room, gripping an unfolded newspaper, another in the hand that maneuvered his cane. He looked unnerved.

"A photograph finally made the dailies." He handed a paper to his grandson.

Malia hurried to Frank's side. Her eyes widened. Sure enough, on the front page was a black-and-white image she'd never seen before or even remembered being taken. Edwin Daly in a dress jacket. Her in the yellow-and-black Jeanne Paquin gown, the one she'd worn to the fund-raiser for the Museum of Art. That was ten months ago. The headline—

Oh, she felt sick.

It said—

ASSISTANT D.A. FIANCÉE MISSING

Mr. Louden's fingers tightened around the paper. "A $1,000 reward is offered for anyone with information leading to her whereabouts."

No one spoke.

Malia took the paper—ripped it, actually—from him. How could anyone think she and Mr. Daly were a couple by this photograph? He faced the camera, posing, but she stood off to the side, clearly talking to someone else. She drew in a calming breath. There was no need to panic. This was a good thing. It had to be, right? That Daly was offering a reward meant the mafiosi still had no idea where she was. Irene and those at the special prosecutor's office who helped her were still safe. No one had been beaten into confessing where she was.

Mrs. Grahame touched Malia's arm. "Darling, you don't look well."

Malia wet her lips nervously and swallowed. "It, uh…I think, uh—" She cut herself off. A panicked chuckle threatened to burst from her throat. Frank would know what to do. She didn't have to worry. He would keep her safe. She waited for him to look her way, for him to tell her everything would be fine, that he had a plan. The seconds stretched, it seemed, into hours.

Malia willed him to look at her. To hold and comfort her. Please.

His hand moved toward hers, then fisted and drew back.

"What do we do now?" Mr. Grahame put in.

"Frank," prodded his grandmother.

"I need—" His jaw shifted. He ran a hand through his hair. "I need to call Henkel." His gaze settled on his grandfather, whose blue eyes mirrored the gravity in his own. "He needs to convince the judge to move up the deposition date. Every day now is one closer to the mafiosi finding her. More than ever, we need to keep Malia hidden." And he strode from the room.

In good news, Worth still sat where Malia had ordered him.

*Grahame Kitchen*
*Day sixteen of twenty-one*
*10:08 a.m.*

Frank leaned against the door frame and looked past his grandfather, the chef and the kitchen maid to the person he desired most to see. Her back to him, Malia stood at the counter cradling a metal bowl. She scraped a wooden spoon around its sides. Since learning of her photo in the papers yesterday, she had said little to him, even while they'd played bridge last night with his grandparents. She seemed sad. No, that wasn't it. Pensive.

He'd leave her alone, but they needed to talk.

He gently tapped the wrapped book he held against his thigh. "You are a hard person to find, when you don't want to be found."

Her gaze stayed on the mixing bowl. "Who said I didn't want to be found?"

"Grandmother."

"Oh."

Grandfather rose from the table by the window. He nodded at Frank then motioned to the chef and kitchen maid at the stove. They left through the serving door. Grandfather walked to Frank, patted his shoulder then left too.

When Malia said no more, Frank put in, "What are you making?"

"Italian cookies. Mr. Grahame didn't believe me when I told him I knew how to cook." Her arm paused in stirring. She drew in a breath then resumed the motion. "Nonna insisted on teaching me all her recipes. She'd say" —her voice pitched higher— "*Someday, little Malia, I may not have servants and live in a fine house, and then who will cook for me?* And I would yell, *I will.* She never expected Nonno's good fortune in America to last."

Frank pushed himself away from the door frame and strolled to the counter. "I'm sorry."

That got her attention. She looked up. "For what?"

"I'm sorry they died and left you alone." Frank slid the paper-wrapped book onto the stacked tin baking sheets on the counter. He watched as the pensive thoughts she'd had for the past twenty-four hours collided in a fury that brightened her eyes. Liquid amber. He'd seen her cry over her circumstances. It was high time for her to get angry.

She dropped the wooden spoon in the bowl that contained a creamy mixture he guessed to be butter, sugar and maybe an egg or two. She then smacked the bowl onto the counter.

"I have my brother who is a notorious gangster and, likely, a murderer." She spoke in a voice colder than he'd ever heard from her. "Nonno and Papà were criminals too, so some would say I am better off with them dead. Don't feel sorry for me, Mr. Louden." She took a step to leave, but he grabbed her wrist and held firm.

"You don't believe that."

"Why shouldn't I?"

"Because they loved you." It was all he could do not to grab her shoulders and shake sense into her. "Something's been nagging at me for the past two weeks. Van Kelly didn't survive in the shadows on his own cleverness. He needed minions to do his dirty work, connections to protect his identity."

Her gaze shifted to his grip.

Frank let go. To his relief she didn't flee.

He rested his hand on a gun hilt. Since they'd arrived in Tuxedo, he hadn't felt the need to be armed. Until this morning. Gut instinct, Holy Spirit impression, he wasn't sure which, but neither was he ignoring the feeling. "Why do you think Van Kelly sent his precious sister to do something that put her directly in danger?"

Her mouth opened, jaw shifted as she tried to form words, to find words. "I— I don't know," she said curtly.

Frank knew, or at least he thought he had her brother's motives figured out. After discussing it earlier that morning with his grandfather, he felt more confident that his hunch—that what he hoped was true—was on target. "He did it because he trusted you more than anyone else."

She blanched. Her gaze fell to the mixing bowl, and a wry chuckle came forth. "There, you're wrong. Giovanni doesn't trust me any more than Papà or Nonno did. He told me about the safe because I'm the only Vaccarelli left alive to help him. Vaccarellis always help one another."

"He could have sent his lawyer."

"No," she countered. "Giovanni insisted he needed him with him at the jail."

"He could have sent one of the coppers he buys off. He could have sent a score of others, but he didn't, Malia." Frank rested his hands gently on her shoulders. She stiffened. "He sent you, the sister he swore to protect, because he loves you and—" He stopped at the spark of pain in her eyes.

But he couldn't stop.

He cared for her too much to not help her see the truth.

He gave her shoulders a little squeeze then lowered his hands. "Giovanni knew exactly what you would do when you found the sourdough."

She looked at him in disbelief. "He knew I would call Irene?"

"Who else in your life will help you without qualms?"

She hesitated. "No one."

*I will,* Frank wanted to yell. She could come to him and he would help her. If he loved her—if she were his—he would cross mountains and deserts and streams for her. "Your brother knew you had no one but your close friend Irene, who just so happens to be a lawyer. When a girl finds counterfeit bills in a family safe in her home, the first thing she needs is a lawyer."

With her fingertips, she rubbed her eyes, shaking her head. "It doesn't make sense. What is it you see and I don't?"

"Tell me what you did after you found the sourdough."

While her look was peeved, it held none of the earlier anger. She drew the wooden spoon back and forth in the butter mixture. "Well, I called Irene because I knew I couldn't go to the family lawyers. I didn't—I couldn't—trust them."

"Then what?"

"Irene suggested we turn the money over to the special prosecutor because I don't trust coppers."

He raised his brows in false indignation. "You don't trust me?"

Another peeved look. "You're different."

"Thank you." Then before she could respond, he added, "I know. It wasn't a compliment."

She tried not to smile.

He didn't smile either. At first.

Frank refocused on his mission. "You didn't know Irene had called the marshal service, so what were you planning on doing next?"

A blush stole across her cheeks. "It was naive of me to think that I could, but, if I hadn't mentioned the list, I would've walked out of that office and returned—" The spoon slid from her hand and banged against the side of the metal bowl.

"Home," he finished. He reached to her cheek. "Eyelash," he said, brushing it off with the side of his thumb. "If you had done that, the mafiosi would have snatched you before you could have made it inside the Waldorf."

She blinked. "I would be in their protective custody."

Or dead. Likely dead, considering she could connect

her brother and four other mafiosi bosses with Mad Dog Miller's death. She wasn't significant enough to keep alive.

"Malia, every action you made that day was you being the good Christian girl you are."

"And you think Giovanni counted on that?"

"You aren't a complex woman."

She dumped the premeasured flour mixture into the mixing bowl. "Your flattery has no bounds."

He loved every ounce of her sarcasm. "Giovanni also counted on a lawyer doing what she should by getting her client protection. Despite how much he hates coppers, he had to know you would be safer with the marshals."

She gripped the bowl with one hand and stirred the mixture, combining the flour with the cream. "Let's say this is true, and I did exactly what Giovanni counted on me doing."

Her head tilted ever so much to the side as she looked at him. And she said something. Or not. Frank wasn't sure beyond that her lips moved. He stared. He couldn't stop. It wasn't her lips or her perfectly shaped face or the sun-kissed glow to her skin. It wasn't even her wit or ability to laugh with abandon, or how she honored and respected his grandparents with no pretense, manipulative flattery or self-interested deception.

He couldn't stop because it was *how* she looked at him. How she looked at everyone on the Grahame estate. Unveiled.

Who Malia Vaccarelli was was there in her eyes. No mysteries. No secrets. Yes, she was beautiful, gloriously beautiful, but it wasn't her beauty that drew people to her, drew him to her. She loved and served and treated others with kindness because doing so was as natural to her as breathing. A woman like her invited a man to love. Invited him to put down his sword and rest. He adored her. He loved—

His breath literally whooshed from his body.

Frank leaned back against the edge of the counter. Two things. That's all he had to do—keep her safe and guard his heart—and he couldn't even accomplish the easiest one.

She touched his arm, concerned. "Frank?"

She looked up at him with such tenderness, such…

Love.

He didn't move. Their bodies weren't touching—thank God for that—but he could feel her warmth radiating off her skin, breathe her simple clean scent from the Ivory soap his grandmother insisted be placed in every washroom. She was so close he could reach out and pull her into his arms and kiss her senseless. His mind raced with images of it. He growled under his breath. His duty was to protect her, not compromise her.

She caught her lower lip between her teeth, an innocent action stemming from her sincere concern, yet it only made him want her more. Frank grabbed the counter with both hands, his palms pressing down onto the cold soapstone. He pressed his eyes closed.

He tried to keep his tone light. "You were saying?" He didn't have to open his eyes to know she was watching him.

"You sound odd."

"I'm fine," he ground out.

After a soft "hmmph," she said, "I asked, 'What is his motive?'"

"You, Malia," he snapped. "You are his motive." He knew because he felt the same. Like Giovanni, he would do anything to protect her, even if it cost him his life. And she wasn't even his; she would never be his. Frank grimaced at what he had to say next.

The truth was going to hurt.

He opened his eyes, met her confused gaze. "This is all

part of Giovanni's plan to force you out of his life because he knows you won't go willingly."

Malia shook her head, unable to breathe from his verbal punch. She refused to believe Giovanni wanted her out of his life. He loved her. They were family. They had only each other.

"Giovanni would never—" She growled under her breath. She wasn't even going to argue the point. "You're wrong, Frank, and I'm not leaving my brother. Ever."

He didn't answer.

He didn't look right. He certainly hadn't sounded normal. Although, he wouldn't have said what he had if his intentions hadn't been good. Frank was the type of person to point out food in your teeth, not to embarrass you, but to spare you from a worse embarrassment of knowing thirty other people saw you. He was considerate like that. Because he cared.

"Maybe you should sit down," she suggested. "Take the weight off your foot."

The stubborn man didn't move. Fine. He could stand there all day, if it made him happy, or miserable. To each his own. She had cookies to bake.

Malia reached around him to grab one of the baking sheets. On top was a package wrapped in butcher paper and tied with twine, and with a comedic pencil drawing of an ice-cream bowl filled with colorful, smiling hearts with faces. "What's this?"

His gaze shifted to the package. "Oh that…ehrm. It's for you."

She blinked. "You bought me a gift. How sweet." And then, because of his sassy words yesterday when she'd been giving her first dog training lesson to his grandmother, she teased, "You did say you were in love. Is this a token of your affection?"

"No," he blurted. His face reddened. "While you were being Grandfather's social secretary this morning, Grandmother asked me to drive her to Wren's Ice Cream Parlor and Sweet Shoppe. It's in the village. The owner is collecting books and donations for the new library. I saw" —he nodded to the package— "that in the box and thought you might like to read it before you leave."

Malia wasn't sure if she should laugh or be mortified. "You stole a book from a donation box? Frank!"

He ran a hand through his hair. "I didn't steal it, all right? I explained to Mr. Wren that a friend of mine was visiting and liked the book, so I asked permission to borrow it. Mr. Wren said it'd be fine. The wrapping was his idea. He likes to draw," he said, tapping the quirky drawing. "I have to give the book back before we leave. In five days. Maybe sooner. You should read quickly."

She looked up at him, assessing his rambling comments. Something ailed him, because…this awkwardness wasn't Frank.

She rested the baking pan atop her mixing bowl. From the corner of her eye, she could see him. He looked everywhere but at her as she untied twine and removed the paper to expose the green cover:

The WONDERFUL WIZARD OF OZ

She pressed her lips together, still looking down at the cover. She brushed her hand across the image of the Scarecrow and Tin Woodman, and the red Lion behind OZ. Frank borrowed this because he'd been thinking about her. And it embarrassed him for her to know. Such a simple gift, and yet she couldn't think of one she treasured more, despite that she had to give it back.

Malia felt herself warming inside. "I don't know what to say."

He shrugged. "A mere 'You are the most considerate man who has ever lived' will suffice."

"Oh, will it?" She couldn't school her smile. "In light of the thoughtfulness of your gift, Mr. Louden, I must confess my reading skills are…well, they aren't expeditious." With both hands, she held the book out to him. "Perchance the most considerate man who has ever lived would read it to me as I finish baking? Chapter four, please."

His head was shaking, but he was grinning. "Sometimes you make me want to—"

"To what?"

Frank snatched the book. Without a hitch in his stride, he walked to the table under the kitchen's middle window. Whatever had been bothering him hadn't been his splinted toe. He took a seat and opened the book.

Malia set the baking pan on the counter as he loudly flipped through pages like a ten-year-old boy being forced to read in front of the class. Giggles bubbled inside. She wouldn't laugh, and risk ruining the moment. In five days, she would return to New York and walk out of Frank's life. Until then, she was going to enjoy every second they had left together.

Using a spoon, she scooped out walnut-size pieces of cookie dough. She rolled each piece of dough into a rope then shaped it into a loop. She laid it on the pan.

"Finally!" he exclaimed. "I was about to think this book was missing a chapter." He cleared his throat. *"When Dorothy awoke the sun was shining through the trees and Toto had long been out chasing birds around him and squirrels."* Something between a snort and a chuckle burst from his chest.

She scooped and formed another cookie. "Care to tell me what's so amusing?"

"Squirrels aren't worth chasing. Toto should have known better."

"Would you have known better?"

He just looked at her.

She looked at him back. "Of course you wouldn't have known better."

"What's that supposed to mean?"

"It's inherent in a male's nature to pursue." She smirked. "Just as it is a female's to want to be caught. Didn't you know birds and squirrels are all female?"

Of all he muttered, she caught only one word: "Women." He resumed reading.

Malia finished rolling the cookies as she listened to Dorothy and the Scarecrow meeting the Tin Woodsman. While the cookies baked during chapter five, the chef and Mary, the kitchen maid, returned to prepare lunch. Malia made coffee and joined Frank at the table for chapter six.

"*'That is a first-rate idea,' said the Lion,*" read Frank. "*One would almost suspect you had brains in your head, instead of straw.*"

"Yes, one would," Malia muttered, cutting in. Then she frowned. "How often do you think we desperately strive for something only to find that, well, we had what we wanted all along?"

He gave her hand a placating pat. "Darling, don't spoil the ending for me."

"What?" she blurted, eyes wide. "You aren't supposed to tell me I figured out the ending."

"What makes you think—" His gaze turned to the door, to the voices growing in volume in the corridor. Frank dropped the book. "Go," he ordered the chef and Mary, and they immediately fled. He stood. "Malia, get up." He grabbed her hand, pulled her around the table and shoved her behind him, shielding her with his body, holding her there with his left arm. His right hand gripped the hilt of his gun.

She didn't have to touch him to feel the tension in his body.

## Chapter 12

It is impossible to play any game without a thorough knowledge of the laws that govern it.

—Emily Price Post, *Etiquette*

The door opened partway.

"Perhaps that is true, but I would love to see him," came a cultured female voice, and Malia released the breath she was holding. Whoever the woman was, she wasn't here for her.

Malia peeked around Frank's shoulder. The door swung open. Inside walked a stately woman, her white hat cocked at an angle over her honey-colored hair; her tightly corseted black dress with vertical white stripes and umbrella skirt defined an hourglass figure. In her right hand, she held an ebony cane with a silver cap handle. Every exquisite inch of her decried High Society. This woman, unlike Malia, hadn't had to read an etiquette book to know to look like a lady. It had been bred into her.

"Hello, Frank," she purred, yet her heavily lidded eyes were on Malia.

His arm lowered, hand released his gun. "Rose." Simply said yet Malia could hear the underlying hostility. Whoever she was, Frank wasn't pleased to see her, which brought Malia a flittering of pleasure.

Mr. and Mrs. Grahame entered, both looking nervous, along with another exquisitely dressed female in an orchid day dress with an ivory lace overlay. She moved past the Grahames to stand next to the other blonde. She looked peeved.

"Katie," Frank drawled in that easygoing voice of his. "It's good to see you."

"I can't say the same, brother dear," she quipped. "What are you doing in the kitchen, and why are you hiding that maid?"

"Miss Leah Carr is Worth's governess," Mrs. Grahame put in. "She is training him. And me, for that matter. Rose, Kate, let's return to the parlor." Lips pursed, she tipped her head to the door with a *you'd better obey me* glare. "Frank, do join us. Rose has returned from England and had the kindness to visit on her way home to Chicago. Has it been seven years already?"

Seven years? Frank's divorce was that long ago. Malia opened her mouth, but Mr. Grahame gave a quick shake of his head, warning her to close it. And she did.

"Come along," chimed Mrs. Grahame.

The woman called Rose kept staring at Malia, as if Malia had shown up to a ball uninvited.

Kate's censorious gaze shifted from Frank to the table with the empty plate, coffee cups and open book. She then looked from Malia back to Frank. Her eyes flared. "Wait, I see what this is," she said icily. "We've interrupted your romantic tête-à-tête."

"Katherine Louden Rainier," implored Mrs. Grahame, "not in front of—"

Kate gave a dismissive wave of her hand. "You and your religious piety have nerve judging me," she said to Frank, "when here you are dallying with a servant. If I had known you were in Tuxedo, I would have never agreed to accompany Rose to see Grandmother. You…are…a…hypocrite."

"Katie, that's enough," Mr. Grahame snapped.

Frank twisted his neck, and Malia heard a pop.

The woman called Rose looked as if she had an epiphany. She grabbed Kate's wrist. "Katie, that's no maid. She's the D.A.'s missing fiancée, the one whose picture is in all the papers. The one for whom the reward has been upped to ten thousand dollars." She chuckled. "I bet someone would pay more than that to know she's here."

In two strides, Frank was standing in front of Rose, his bearing that of a military man. Malia couldn't see his face, but his sister blanched and took a step back. His grandmother gripped her husband's arm.

"You will not tell a soul where she is."

Rose flinched.

His words—they were harsh, no doubt about it—held a power that reminded Malia of the story in Acts when the Apostle Paul confronted Elymas the false prophet for perverting the straight ways of the Lord. But this wasn't a spiritual battle. This was…well, it wasn't a battle at all. She wasn't the prize. Nor did her honor need defending.

There was perfect silence.

Then a curve grew on Rose's lips. "Impressive."

"We need to talk." Frank grabbed his sister's arm and one of Rose's and pulled them out of the kitchen.

Mrs. Grahame looked to Malia, eyes filled with compassion. "Will you be all right?"

She nodded.

Mr. Grahame hesitated. With a sigh, he clenched his wife's hand and left Malia in the kitchen. Alone.

*Grahame Library*
*Later that afternoon*

With the tip of her little finger, Malia smeared the charcoal cloud in her sketch for Mr. Grahame. A man who treasured the memory of flying a kite with his grandchildren should have a picture to remember it. Especially a man who had personally searched the house to find his oldest grandson's sketchbook and charcoals because his youngest grandson had mentioned she enjoyed drawing. As she sat on the window seat listening to the lively orchestra music softly playing from the Gramophone, she glanced at the lake resting peacefully on the other side of the glass. Since Frank's sister and ex-wife arrived, she'd seen little of him, or of his grandparents. She missed them, and it had been only four hours.

That she missed them didn't mean she was lonely.

She wasn't lonely. She had a brother. She had a dear friend, who was also her lawyer, and she had artists she sponsored. She knew practically everyone who volunteered at the Museum of Art. She couldn't ride down a Manhattan street without seeing someone she knew. Her life was full of people she spoke with daily. She had events to attend, charities to aid. She wasn't lonely.

*This is all part of Giovanni's plan to force you out of his life because he knows you wouldn't go willingly.*

Frank wouldn't have said that if he hadn't thought it was true. But why would Giovanni want her out of his life? He loved her—of that she had no doubt. When she visited him in the jail, he'd specifically said everything he was doing was to protect her. She trusted him to do just that. She would stay in New York during the trial. She would visit him in jail. She wasn't leaving him. Ever. Because when you loved someone, you didn't leave.

A knock resounded on the door frame.

Malia looked up.

Frank stood there, smiling. "Might I have permission to ruin your solitude?"

She nodded. "Where are Mrs. Rainier and Mrs. Swaine Louden Bingham?" Two weeks ago, she'd desperately wanted to be accepted by Society women like Frank's sister and ex-wife. Something in her had changed. Wealth did not make one part of the Best Society of people. Good character did. She'd rather join the working class than go back to that world.

"They just left to take Grandmother and Grandfather into the village for an ice-cream sundae." He walked to the Gramophone, turned the hand crank, and moved the needle to the beginning of the record. "I'm sorry for earlier."

"I can think of worse unexpected arrivals."

He, strangely, didn't smile. "Katie hates me."

Malia nodded. Really, what did one say in response to that?

"I've never lectured or condemned my sister for her indiscretions," he said, walking to Malia. "Accusing me of doing so is easier than accepting that the shame she feels is from her own conscience." He sat on the other end of the window seat.

"After the divorce, my family tried to console me. *It's not your fault. The affair was Rose's choice. She was the one who left.* None of that mattered. I ignored my family, focused on finishing my law degree because…"

He turned and gazed out the window, his blue eyes lightened by the bright afternoon sun.

Malia closed the sketchbook's cover and returned the charcoal to the box. In the past four hours, she'd been so selfishly wallowing in her own woes that she had not given a thought to how his ex-wife's arrival made him feel. She couldn't feel any lower.

He turned back to her. "For years whenever I looked at people who knew about Rose and me, I saw the same judgment in their eyes—*unclean*."

His words cut deep. When he'd walked into the special prosecutor's office, that's how she'd felt. Had he truly looked at her as if she was unclean, or, as with his sister Katie, had her own shame done the accusing?

She grabbed a cloth and wiped her coal-tipped fingers. "One of the artists I sponsor is a divorcée, whom none of the other patrons wanted. Her church even asked her to leave." Malia laid the cloth atop the sketchbook. "She said she felt like a leper. People she thought were friends treated her like she was contagious."

"I felt like I'd lost a part of my soul. Divorce left me broken, but that broken part of me is what let Jesus in." He spoke so matter-of-factly that she ached over his pain. His frown deepened. "While Rose, Katie and I were talking earlier, I knew I needed to tell Rose I forgave her."

"That must have been difficult."

"It felt like my soul was being ripped in half." He rested his head against the wood-paneled wall. His voice tightened. "Then I realized that pain was God stitching me whole. I wished her well, and meant it."

"Everybody needs grace."

He shifted on the bench. That familiar smile of his returned. "Some people find grace easier to give than others do. I'm trying to be more like you."

This man—this God-fearing, family-honoring man—was what she used to dream of marrying. *I want a good man,* had been her prayer for years. She wasn't in love with him, not that she knew what being in love felt like. She'd never been in love before. But if she let herself fall in love, if she let Frank into her heart, he was a man she would love until the day she died.

The bitter medicine was that he couldn't love her. No, he could, but he wouldn't. She wasn't the best thing for him. Frank had all the opportunities to live her dream of the perfect life with the right spouse. He had career aspirations with the marshal service. He'd practically glowed when he'd told her about the possibility of becoming chief marshal of the Southern District of New York. He had family he loved and who loved him. Malia Vaccarelli would never be welcomed in his world.

"You're a good man, Frank Louden." She paused. "I pray one day you find a woman who treasures what Rose tossed away."

He looked at her with some surprise. Then his gaze grew warm, hot, and for a moment, she almost believed he wanted…her. It couldn't be. It was only her own desire making her see what she wanted, which was…him. She wanted him to be her protector, not as a marshal but as a husband and a friend. And she wanted to protect him too because she—

Her breath caught. Because she loved him. Because she had let him into her heart.

And it hurt.

Eyes blurring, Malia rested her head against the windowpane. Five days. All she had to do was get through the next five days without letting him know, without ruining the friendship they'd built. She could do it. She closed her eyes and breathed deep as her racing pulse slowed, as the sun warmed her face, as she accepted her feelings and what could never be.

She opened her eyes. The day was made to be outside. Run through the grass. Lie in the sun. Skip rocks in the lake. Chase squirrels like Worth. Worth!

Malia shifted onto her knees, palms flat on the glass,

panicking. She'd assumed Mrs. Grahame had taken him with her. What was he doing outside?

"Frank, Worth just ran into the woods!"

Before Frank could tell Malia she'd probably seen a rabbit or fawn enjoying the spring day, she dashed from the library. He looked out the window. Nothing but trees, rocks and foliage. No white Pomeranian thinking it was a fox with the skills to catch a squirrel, which was only logical because he'd seen his grandmother get into the Studebaker with the dog in her lap. Hadn't he?

He left the library, asking each person he saw which way Malia had run. By the time he stepped out the summer entrance, he could not see Malia, the dog nor any other animal.

"That way," the footman said, pointing to the west woods.

Frank took off jogging in that direction. He maneuvered around several shrubs on the hilly woodland and over a half-knocked-down, moss-covered rock wall. Malia was not to be seen or heard in the forest. He took care descending the first slope. Brace hand against bark. Step over wedged rock in the ground. Don't slide on composting leaves. His last adventure in these woods—chasing after Worth, who had been chasing after a squirrel—had resulted in a broken toe. It was bad enough Malia was chasing the wrong animal, but considering the underbrush, her chances were good for finding a poisonous snake or—

The faint pounding of hammers pulled him up short.

Immigrant workers. Italians. Slavs. Hundreds of them were working on the cottage up the hill. Hundreds with access to the dailies. His mind reeled. Any one of them could recognize her.

Frank took off running. He scrambled up the embankment and through the thick woods, his pulse racing, mind

besieged with fear. Why hadn't he warned Malia to stay
out of the woods? Rose was right. With a ten-thousand-
dollar reward being offered, anyone who had Malia would
be wise to keep her hidden until the reward was doubled.
Tripled, even. Her life meant nothing to a kidnapper.

Not again. He couldn't go through that again.

Frank exited the woods. His feet froze, but his pulse
raced.

She wasn't here.

A score of men next to a wagon full of boards spoke
loud and in Italian. One looked Frank's way. He tapped the
man next to him, and then the group parted. Malia stood
in the middle talking to a worker and Charlie Patterson,
who held Worth tucked snugly under his arm. Frank felt
himself choking. All his precautions ruined by a dog. It
was everything he could do not to raise his gun and demand they all step back, but he couldn't do it. He couldn't
do anything to arouse their suspicions that she wasn't just
a servant from a neighboring estate chasing after a run-
away pet. He couldn't let them know that he was chasing
after her.

His palms fisted to stop the trembling, to stop the shaking inside. Breathe. He had to breathe.

Charlie yelled to the men to get back to work. Before
they did, each one took turns gallantly shaking Malia's
hand. Charlie finally pulled her away from the group.
That's when she looked Frank's way. The color in her
cheeks drained from her face.

She and Charlie ambled over as if they didn't have a
care in the world and stopped before Frank.

"I found Worth with the workers," she said with cheer
and a smile he knew was for his benefit. "Superintendent
Patterson appeared like magic. The workers called him
*Come il Vento* because, like the wind, he always seems to
be everywhere in the park."

Charlie blushed. He looked to Frank. "She told them she was a recent immigrant who spoke nothing but Italian and was so thankful to be in America."

She looked to Charlie. "I worried I was a bit too exuberant in my newfound patriotism."

"You were convincing." He turned to Frank. "If I hear anything suspicious, I'll let you know." He gave Malia the dog. "Take care, Miss Carr."

"Thank you again," she answered.

Charlie returned to the worksite, and Frank fell into step with Malia, the only sound an occasional broken twig and his rough breathing. And the dog—he smelled. Frank followed as Malia led him on a path through the woods to a grassy rock-covered hillside easier to traverse than where he'd come through.

"You're rather silent," Malia put in.

"You didn't have to chase the dog," Frank snapped as they reached where the ground leveled and the woods turned into his grandparents' grassy lawn.

Malia stopped. "I think I preferred your silence."

"He would have returned eventually."

"Considering what Worth means to your grandmother, I couldn't take the risk."

"You should have," he bit off, his heart still racing and blood pounding. He shouldn't have yelled. She didn't realize the danger she put herself in. He cared about the dog's safety, but not as he cared about hers. "You have to stop being so naive as to believe everyone has good intentions. Stop being a woman who takes candy from strangers."

She released a loud, I-am-losing-my-patience-with-you sigh. "What has come over you?"

He'd known from the beginning she would do something foolish. "All it takes is for one of those workers to see a photo in the dailies and recognize you."

"They're poor workers, Frank. They don't simply hop on the first train to Manhattan whenever they like."

"They can use a phone."

She rolled her eyes then resumed walking to the house.

"In five days anything could happen," he called out.

"It won't."

Frank ran to catch up with her. "I'm taking precautions for your safety."

"A person can't take precautions to prevent every bad thing." She stopped at the summer entrance. "What about discovering your brother is a gangster? Or learning your life is a facade? Or being told your brother wants you out of his life? What precautions could I have taken to prevent those things from happening?"

The pain in her eyes—it was like looking at Katie. He couldn't end her pain any more than he could help his sister.

He looked burdened. Wrecked. Malia knew the fault was hers. In hindsight, chasing after Worth hadn't been the wisest of ideas. She could have waited a bit and if Worth hadn't returned, she could have sent a footman. In her selfish need to rescue Worth, she hadn't considered how her action would hurt Frank, just as she hadn't thought how involving Irene would put her in danger.

Malia stepped closer. "I'm sorry. Today is my day for blundering, it seems." She drew in a breath and cringed. Worth smelled foul. "Can we talk later? I need to bathe Worth before your grandmother returns."

He nodded.

She hurried inside and up the stairs to the bathroom used by guests who didn't have one en suite. She set Worth down in the claw-foot tub.

"Sit," she ordered. He did but trembled. She knelt on

the rug then gave him a treat from her apron pocket. "I'm sorry. I'll make this as painless as possible."

In moments he was soaked.

"Malia, I need to tell you something."

She jerked her head toward Frank standing next to the door she'd forgotten to close. "You can't be in here. Go," she said, waving a bar of soap at him.

He stepped off the tile floor and into the wood-planked hallway.

She glared at him.

He didn't leave.

Face warming, Malia focused on lathering Worth.

"Katie was kidnapped when she was thirteen," he said matter-of-factly.

She stared at him. No one had said anything.

"We were on holiday at the beach," he went on. "That summer Mother decided the best way to teach Katie and me to get along was to make us do things together."

"Mamma did the same."

"Did it work?"

She thought for a moment. "No," she said, scrubbing Worth's belly. "We didn't stop bickering until I left for Vassar."

"I wish I could say Katie and I stopped." He paused. "No, that's not true. I did after we got her back."

She wasn't surprised. Losing a loved one—or almost losing—had to change a person's thinking.

"We were tasked with procuring sarsaparillas from a vendor. I was angry because I wanted lemonade, but Katie—" He shook his head. "Katie always got what she wanted. So when this man stopped her and asked for directions, I didn't wait for her. I walked away. Our parents received ransom demands cautioning against going to the police on threat of her life. Every time Father went to make the exchange, the kidnappers failed to appear."

Unable to grasp the magnitude of how his family—how he—felt, Malia began rinsing Worth, who didn't like the water yet obediently sat. "How did you get her back? Did she escape?"

"Grandfather contacted a friend who was a judge. He immediately brought in the marshals. They found her."

Malia turned off the water with one hand and held Worth down with the other to keep him from shaking. She nodded to the towels stacked neatly on a bench under the tall window. "Could you…?"

Frank quickly claimed one for her. He held it open, then looked down and clearly realized he was inside the bathroom. Before she could say anything, he wrapped the towel around Worth, scooped him up and hurried back into the hall. Malia grabbed a second towel. They walked to the sitting room at the top of the stairs. Frank sat on the sofa in front of the set of three cathedral windows and held Worth as Malia dried him.

"Is that why you became a marshal?" she asked.

He nodded. "Marshal Henkel called while I was talking with Katie and Rose. Edwin Daly has been indicted. The deposition has been moved up to tomorrow. It's time to leave Oz, Dorothy, but" —he scratched Worth's head— "little Toto here gets to stay." He was attempting to lighten the mood; she knew him too well.

Something flickered in his eyes. Something he didn't want her to see. Something he was hiding. For him to hide anything from her meant the news wasn't good. It had to be about her brother, or Irene, or any of the people she'd spoken to that day.

Malia swallowed, trying to calm the sudden pounding in her chest. She moistened her lips. When she spoke again, her voice was rough. "Who is it?"

He looked at her, all innocent. "Who is what?"

"Don't play dumb, Frank Louden," she snapped. "Who's been hurt?"

"Irene."

Malia drew in a sharp breath. "How did it—"

"She's not dead," he blurted. "The mafiosi have been following her for weeks. My partner Winslow has been protecting her, but last night they got the jump on him. Irene took a few hits before Winslow ran them off. They said if she doesn't stop you from testifying, you will both die. Starting with her."

# Chapter 13

Exhibitions of anger, fear, hatred, embarrassment, ardor or hilarity, are all bad form in public.
—Emily Price Post, *Etiquette*

*Tweed Courthouse*
*Manhattan Island*
*April 26, 1901*

Animals in a zoo—that's what she and Giovanni were to them.

Malia watched their audience—five standing in a row along the wall while she and Giovanni sat across from each other at the table in the center of the conference room. Frank, his hand resting on a gun hilt. Irene dressed defiantly in a red day dress despite a swollen lip and black eye. Flanking them…Special Prosecutor Cady; Giovanni's lawyer, Mr. Sirica; and Chief Marshal Henkel. As a consequence of her meeting with Giovanni at the police department seventeen days ago, no appeal to the judge could earn them a private reunion. Frank's meager proficiency in Dutch granted him access, since none of the rest of their audience could speak it. Who knew how many others were, somehow, listening in.

Only she and Giovanni were people, not animals, who had lives that had been destroyed because—oh, the irony of it all—fifty-six years ago Antonio Vaccarelli and his new bride immigrated to New York in their pursuit of the American Dream. Nonno's dream, though, had been to honor his father's request he expand Sicily's Old World mafiosi into the New World.

"Aren't you going to ask me if I killed Mad Dog Miller?" Giovanni stretched his arms across the table.

Malia gripped his cuffed hands. "I don't want to know if you killed him, or anyone," she answered honestly. "Knowing won't lessen my love for you."

He smiled somewhat. While Giovanni had no bruises that she could see, his face was leaner. Whatever food he'd been living on in jail wasn't crab cakes and steak. Between his oversize white-and-black bee-striped uniform and her white lace dress with the soot-stained hem, they looked nothing like the *nouveau riche* they were.

Her heart tightened. Pride did go before destruction. A haughty spirit did go before a fall.

Giovanni's dark brows drew together. "You look petrified."

"I am. For you."

"Don't be." His gaze drifted for but a second to their audience. "Malia," he said in a gentle voice, "everything I have done is to protect you. I need you to understand that everything I do next is to protect you."

Frank cleared his throat.

Malia's uneasiness grew even more. She looked to

Frank, and he gave her a look simple to read: ask him. Frank was right. She needed to know the truth. But if she wasn't careful, she could make things worse for Giovanni.

She leveled her chin, keeping her gaze high despite the weakness she felt. "You knew all along what I would do."

The corner of his mouth indented. "You are…predictable."

Her body went still. Those three insignificant words spoke what he couldn't directly say. But she knew. Her breathing grew ragged, choking. Her head shook. Lips pursed, trembled. He had judged her life and found her to be honest and true, just as a proper, Christian woman should be. He knew she would be faithful too. He knew she wouldn't leave him unless he took away her ability to stay. Tears flooded her eyes. She wanted to live free, not behind glass walls or social exclusivity. She wanted something abundant and true, and she wanted her brother to be a part of her life. Not alone. She couldn't be alone.

She clung to his hands. "You can't do this to me, Giovanni," she cried. "You can't make me go."

"You have to."

"No!" she sobbed, her heart shattering like glass. "I'm not leaving you."

"Yes. You. Will," he ordered. "You will leave New York."

A hand rested on her shoulder, a handkerchief hanging down. Frank.

Malia gasped at the air, desperate to control her breathing. She took his offering, but didn't look at him. She couldn't risk doing anything that could earn him censure because she'd fallen in love with him. Instead of walking back to his place with their audience, Frank moved to the side wall. A mere three feet from her. He looked at her: *Are you all right?*

She gave a little shrug. She tried to smile as she dried her face.

Giovanni looked to Frank. "Are you the one who protected my sister?"

"Yes," came the flat reply.

"Thank you." Giovanni let go of Malia and extended a hand—both actually, considering his wrists were cuffed together. He and Frank shook hands.

"Malia," Giovanni said, turning back to her, "I've done things I'm not proud of. The consequences, here and in eternity, are mine to bear. But I didn't kill Mad Dog. I went to warn him. He was dead when I arrived." He reached for her hands again. "One of us has to have a future, and that is why I've agreed to plea-bargain. The dailies have been notified, so the mafiosi will know soon, if they don't already. You are free not to testify. You can provide no information that I can't as well. Go, start a new life with nothing holding you in the mire."

She stared, shocked. "Why are you doing this?"

For a second his controlled composure cracked. Then what tears welled in his eyes were blinked away. "Because Grandfather DeWitt asked me to not let what happened to Mamma, Papà and our nonni happen to you."

Grandfather DeWitt? He'd known about the Vaccarellis' involvement in the mafiosi? He'd known and she hadn't? Indignation unsettled her. She should not have been the last to know. She had a right to be involved in the decision making. She wasn't a pet who sat upon command.

*Forgive as you've been forgiven. Love as you are loved.*

Malia swallowed to ease the tightness in her throat. God did command her to love and forgive. By the look in Giovanni's blue-gray eyes, she knew he wanted neither her advice nor approval. She couldn't control how he lived his life. And she had no right to force her choices—

her faith—on him. She did have the choice to believe God was accomplishing His purposes in every circumstance.

She looked to the special prosecutor. "Sir, what does his future hold?"

"Sentencing is next week," he answered. "I expect up to twenty years for money laundering and possession of counterfeit currency. He'll be kept in isolation for his protection, and/or transferred to a federal penitentiary. Either Leavenworth or McNeil Island."

She nipped at her bottom lip. Leavenworth was in Kansas, but McNeil Island? She'd never heard of it but no matter where he went, she would find him.

Malia raised Giovanni's hands to her lips and pressed a kiss. "I love you, and I want your life to go well. If this is what you feel is right, then I am praying it all works out well. I will find you again. We're family. Nothing you do—or don't do—will change my love for you."

As Malia and her brother said goodbyes, Henkel clucked his tongue, drawing Frank's attention. He tapped his watch then motioned to the ceiling, the message clear. Once Frank had finished attending to Malia, Henkel wanted to see him upstairs in his office.

Frank nodded, although he didn't know yet what he was going to do with Malia.

Still gripping the handkerchief he gave her, Malia walked with her shoulders held high to Irene, who immediately grabbed Malia's hand. Henkel opened the door for them.

The moment they stepped into the hallway, Cady walked to Frank. "Excellent job, Louden." They shook hands. Cady then took a seat at the table.

The lawyer Sirica pulled an envelope out of his coat pocket and met Frank at the door. He shook Frank's hand

and gave him the envelope, saying, "See that she arrives safely."

Safely? He released a wry chuckle. He should have expected something like this. Giovanni Vaccarelli had been too diligent thus far in orchestrating events. He wouldn't stop now that his sister was free to go. Frank opened the envelope. In block handwriting were detailed instructions that brought a sickening in his stomach and an ache in his heart. At the bottom of the paper was Giovanni Vaccarelli's bold signature. Frank looked over his shoulder to the prisoner, who was looking at him instead of listening to what Special Prosecutor Cady was saying.

He and Vaccarelli leveled stares.

And then Frank nodded.

Irene and Malia were clinging to each other when Frank arrived at the courthouse door where he and Malia had entered only two hours earlier.

"Will we ever see each other again?" Malia was asking. There was an acceptance in her tone that hadn't been there earlier.

"I'd like that, but" —Irene's voice cracked— "how will I know where to find you?"

Using his handkerchief, Malia wiped Irene's tears. "I will find you. I'm so sorry you were hurt because of me."

"I have been blessed to call you friend." Irene smiled then looked to Frank. "Do you have the instructions for where to take her?"

He gave her a rather assessing stare. "You know?"

She nodded. "Three months after Giovanni and I began courting, he shared his intentions because he didn't want our feelings for each other to deepen without me knowing the truth," she said and paid no mind to Malia's wide eyes and gaping mouth. "He asked for my help. By that point, Malia had become like a sister, and I knew I couldn't say no. We continued the charade of courting for another three months." Her bruised chin trembled. "I thought I was prepared for this day."

Frank understood. He, too, had known his time with Malia was limited. No one could prepare for the pain of letting go of a loved one. He waited patiently as the ladies made their final goodbyes, as Malia reassured Irene that she was going to be all right.

Irene rested her hands on each side of Malia's head. She rose on her tiptoes and placed a kiss on her forehead. "God is forever watching over you." And then she returned down the hallway whence they came, leaving Malia and Frank alone beside the door.

Malia patted her eyes dry. "Where does the yellow road lead this time?"

Frank swallowed. It did little to ease the lump in his throat. "Would you like to go see the Wizard?"

"If I say yes, who does that make you on my journey?"

The Tin Woodsman, to be sure. Because until he met her, he'd forgotten what it was like to have a heart. One he wished he could rip from his chest because that would hurt less than being in love. He motioned to the door. "I'm just Toto, along for the journey."

He ushered her out of the courthouse and into a covered carriage where Norma Hogan waited with a change of hat and coat for Malia. Frank whispered instructions to the driver then climbed inside on the seat opposite Malia. Stupid. Torturous. But he wasn't letting her out of his sight until he absolutely had to.

They drove around Manhattan for an hour, both he and Norma checking to see if anyone followed. They turned onto Broadway, already packed with trolley cars, automobiles and horse-drawn carriages, some larger, some smaller than the one they rode in.

Frank could stall no more. He gave the driver the pre-arranged signal to take them to the DeWitt home. They continued to transverse Manhattan in no logical order. If anyone had been trailing them from the courthouse, they'd have surely lost the trail.

As soon as they pulled up to the pale limestone mansion, Malia drew her gaze from the window. "Why are we…here?"

Frank focused on the carriage wall behind her. "This is where your brother asked me to bring you." How he got the words past the lump in his throat, he didn't know.

Norma Hogan closed her book and set it on the bench between them. She took Malia's left hand between hers. "I am honored to have met you."

Malia smiled. "I feel the honor is all—"

The driver opened the door, and Frank jumped out of the carriage with a "Stay here, Malia."

Norma must have been hard on his heels because she stood beside him in an instant. "We weren't followed."

"I know." With Norma watching his every move, Frank pasted a smile on his face and returned to Malia. He swept his arm in an arc. "Milady."

Malia didn't move. "I—I, uh, don't think I can see him after all…." She worried her bottom lip, her beauty mark tormenting him. Was it wrong that here, in front of Norma, Gulian DeWitt, a carriage driver and God himself, all Frank wanted to do was kiss those lips? Claim this beautiful woman as his own? Forsake his family, his fortune and everything he'd been working toward just to be with her?

Yes, yes and yes.

Frank rested his foot on the carriage step. "You can. You have strength and a character that did not shatter upon discovering the truth about your family. Circumstances bend you, but you don't break. I saw that in Cady's office. I saw that in Tuxedo. I saw it at the courthouse earlier." He spoke the words for his benefit as much as for hers.

She looked to the house. The sound of a door opening was accompanied by her eyes widening in fear.

The pain of losing her paled in that moment. "Malia, look at me."

She did.

"You've had twenty-five years of being taught one thing about your grandfather. He isn't going to change your mind" —he pointed over his shoulder— "the moment you walk in that door. Just give him the benefit of the doubt like you gave me. Please."

Malia's eyes teared up, but she stepped out of the carriage. "Thank you. For everything." She walked past without the customary handshake as though she, too, could not bear to touch him, knowing it would be the breaking point.

Norma shook her head, an exasperated look on her face, and took Malia's spot inside the carriage.

Frank looked over his shoulder for one final glance of Malia wrapped in her grandfather's arms. He'd done it. He'd kept her safe. He had returned her home stronger than she was when he found her. They'd said their goodbyes, and he managed not to fall to his knee and profess his undying love. He was a marshal, she a witness. He'd done the right and honorable thing. And it felt as if his heart was being chipped away like ice.

It was time for him to go.

"Tweed Courthouse," he said to the driver before climbing into the carriage. He settled in the seat across from Norma.

She turned the page in the book. "You okay?"

"Yes," he said as the carriage started into motion.

"Did you tell her you love her?"

"What?"

"Did you kiss her?"

"No, why do you even ask that?" he bit off. He rested his head against the back wall. "She was in protective custody. My custody. To kiss her would have crossed the lines of propriety." Although the amount of time he had spent imagining kissing her had to have crossed the lines of propriety too. "While Malia is probably all a man could want in a wife—"

"You mean *you*," Norma cut in. He must have been glaring because she held her hands up defensively. "It's not offensive to call something what it is."

"She is also the sister of a criminal," he continued his argument. "She has no future in New York. Mine is here. We could never have a life together."

Norma shrugged. "You're a good man, Frank."

"Thank you."

She gave him a peeved look.

"So that's not a compliment?" The normal teasing between them reset his equilibrium. He could do this. He could go back to being Frank Louden, deputy marshal, soon to be chief marshal of the Southern District.

Norma returned her attention to her book. "I can't decide if you are more noble than I thought or more stupid."

## Chapter 14

So long as Romance exists…love at first sight and marriage in a week is within the boundaries of possibility. But usually (and certainly more wisely) a young man is for some time attentive to a young woman before dreaming of marriage.

—Emily Price Post, *Etiquette*

*Broad Street Station*
*Philadelphia*
*A month later*

Malia stared in awe at the bas-relief sculpture in the station lobby. While at Vassar, she had seen photographs of Karl Bitter's *The Spirit of Transportation,* but the photos did not do justice to the artistic procession of modes of transportation from covered wagons to a child holding a model of an airplane. Grandfather drew up beside her. She glanced over at him, but his attention was on the sculpture. In his three-piece suit, and with a ruddy face and white hair (what there was of it) and mustache, he was as distinguished-looking as a British colonel of the old school.

"Amazing, isn't it?" he said.

"For the craft of the sculptor alone," she answered, "but the artistry...well, this is quite visionary for work created only six years ago."

He handed her a ticket stub. "Are you sure this is where you want to go?"

Malia slid the ticket into her clutch. With Giovanni transferred to McNeil Island, Washington State and its rain forests, stately mountains, Puget Sound and lack of flying monkeys was the closest she could get to Oz. Having donated her inheritance to the Museum of Art, she had limited funds (though, not if Grandfather had his say), no means of employment and only a letter of reference from the Grahames. Yet her toes literally itched in her shoes in desire to run to the private coach Grandfather had secured. Living in Seattle would be an adventure.

The only thing that could make it better would be having Frank experience it with her.

"Yes, it is," she finally said. "I want to feel the breeze on my face after it's skipped across the waters, and I want to forget all I've left behind in New York. Save you, of course."

He stared at her. "Are you in love with him?"

Malia felt the blood drain from her face. "Who?"

"The marshal. The one to whose family you've been writing letters." Before he gave her a chance to admit or deny it, he said, "Yes, I know about them. I spoke to the Grahames at the opera." The very one she wanted to attend last week but did not dare. "They enjoyed having you visit."

She plucked at the black-braided trim on her royal blue traveling jacket, unable to think of a plausible denial. They had vowed to be honest with each other. And since she would never see Frank again, she confessed, "I thought my feelings would have ended by now."

"Can a person fall out of love quickly?" His words were gentle. "Give it time."

She grinned. "Time? Oh, Grandfather, have you not heard? Out west there is an elixir for it. Granted it is green, tastes like a dog's bathwater and gives one spots, but I would think those are inconsequential to being cured."

He tapped the tip of her nose. "You are too much like your mother." He wrapped her arm around his, and they fell into step, maneuvering around the crowded and noisy station.

"You don't have to come with me," she offered.

"I do." As he had been doing much of since she arrived at his house a month ago, he smiled broadly. "I have five grandsons and one granddaughter. Let me dote on her."

*Tuxedo Park*
*Mid-June*

"Golf requires two things" —Grandfather lined his club up to the ball on the tee— "courage and the ability to keep your eye on the ball." He swung and sent his ball sailing... way left. His new golf knickers clearly weren't his good-luck charm. Not that the pair he'd insisted Frank wear were any luckier for *him*. He was just off his game.

Frank handed his club to his caddy, a son of one of the villagers. "Is this supposed to encourage me to improve my game? 'Cause your score is ten points higher than Katie's and four worse than mine."

"Hmmph," Katie murmured, yet if he didn't know better, he'd swear she was smiling. While she had vocalized her refusal to join Grandfather and Frank in a golf match, her competitive streak overcame her abhorrence at being within three feet of Frank. Or she just wanted the new Oldsmobile Grandfather promised to buy the winner. In her sweeping tweed skirt, blue-and-white-striped shirt and straw boater, she looked every bit the faux enthusiast.

What he hadn't counted on was her actual skill. His sister had an Olympic swing.

Grandfather gave his club to his young caddy George, who, like Frank's and Katie's caddies (strangely also named George), had volunteered at the first offer of a quarter. Grandfather accepted his proffered cane then took off in the direction of his ball. Frank and Katie followed suit.

"He had the drawing Miss Vaccarelli did framed," Katie said, her arms clasped behind her back as they walked. "It's in the library, if you haven't seen it."

Frank hadn't. He'd been conscripted into the golf match within an hour of his arrival for the "reunion weekend" his grandmother insisted on having now that his parents had returned from Paris and Worthing was engaged and wanted to introduce his fiancée to the family. Katie's husband, Augustus, declined to attend. Katie didn't seem bothered, but rarely did Katie share her pain with the family.

A breeze blew across the lawn, fluttering Katie's skirt. Sun overhead, sky bright with an occasional white puff of cloud, and the scent of evergreen in the air—it was another beautiful day in the park, albeit a bit muggy. With most Tuxedo-ites in Europe for the summer, they had the golf course to themselves.

"Is Malia's drawing the one of us flying kites when we were children?" he asked, trying to remember what he'd seen in Worthing's old sketchbook that their grandfather had given her to use.

She nodded.

"I think that was the only time we didn't fight."

Katie nodded again. Then she sighed. "I've heard them speak more praises of Miss Vaccarelli than they ever did of me. I should be jealous, but—" She shrugged. "Have you seen her since?"

Since he left her at her grandfather's? Frank shook his head. "I can't see her."

She stopped him in the middle of the lawn. "Can't? Or won't?" She motioned to their caddies to continue on.

Frank lifted his flat cap and ran a hand through his hair. "It's complicated."

Her gaze shifted to where Grandfather was standing in a bunker and talking to his caddy. "He sat me down in the library last night and lectured me for an hour. He says I'm miserable and it's my own fault, not yours, not Augustus's."

Frank put his cap back on his head. "What happened to you *was* my fault. I didn't protect you like a brother should."

Her jaw shifted. "I'm tired of being angry all the time. I'm tired of being a disappointment to everyone. I am so tired of hating you."

He rested the back of his hand against her palm, enough of a touch to have that connection but not too much to make her uncomfortable. "I want the best for your life, and I would do whatever I need to help you. Nothing you do will ever lessen my love for you."

Her fingers tightened around his. "What about you? Do you want the best for your life?"

Her question jolted him. Of course, he wanted that.

"During Grandfather's lecture," she went on, "he told me goals are a good thing, but in light of doors God opens, I needed to stop being someone who spat in the face of God and said *no, I have my own agenda.* He said you needed to do that, too. Is becoming chief marshal something you want, or is it something you think you need to prove something to yourself? And to Dad?"

Frank looked over her shoulder to the trees framing the course. He needed to earn the promotion to prove he was the best marshal he could be. Every morning he went to work, did his job and came home to an empty apartment. He wasn't lonely…when he was working.

"Katie, I need to know something."

She looked at him expectantly.

"What do you want to come home to at the end of the day?"

Her eyes held a haunted longing. "Someone who loves me."

"What if that meant giving up your life here?"

"Having someone to love and protect me is all I've ever wanted." Then as if embarrassed at her honesty, she resumed walking to Grandfather, and Frank fell into step. "What about you? What do you want to come home to at the end of the day?"

"Malia."

"Then I suppose you have to decide if loving a woman and being a husband and a father fills the void in your life that you think being chief marshal of New York will."

*DeWitt Conservatory*
*Manhattan Island*
*Late June*

Frank sipped his coffee and patiently waited for Gulian DeWitt to pose the next question. Every evening for the past eight days, he'd arrived at precisely 7:00 p.m. for dinner. They would eat, and then precisely at 8:00 p.m., they would retire to the glass-ceiling conservatory for coffee. After explaining what had occurred while Malia was in his protective custody, Frank had talked about his job and his wish to marry. Malia's name hadn't been mentioned then. In the past three days, alone, her name hadn't been mentioned at all. If DeWitt suspected Frank's intentions, he had yet to say anything.

The sounds of the water spilling from the Grecian fountain echoed across the marble tile, the only light in the room provided by the chandelier over the seating area. The potted palms and wicker furniture seemed more suited for a lady's tea time than two men evaluating each other's worth. Although in the cool of the evening, the moderate temperature in the room was a welcome relief after a sweltering afternoon.

DeWitt sat on the sofa next to Frank's chair. He relaxed against the back, one leg crossed over the other. "So you want to marry my granddaughter," DeWitt said without fanfare.

So much for thinking the man didn't suspect Frank's motives.

Frank set his cup on the matching wicker coffee table. "Yes, sir, I do."

"Have you told your parents and grandparents of the seriousness of your intentions?"

"I have."

DeWitt sipped his coffee, his appraising gaze never leaving Frank. He looked nothing like Malia, for which Frank was glad. "Go on."

"Sir, while my grandparents have given their approval, my parents don't feel this is the wisest course of action, considering they have not had the pleasure of meeting your granddaughter, and, to be candid, they feel my decision is emotion-driven."

"Is it?"

"Yes, sir." Frank shifted in the wicker chair that no one in his right mind would find comfortable. He suspected that was DeWitt's reason for choosing this room for their after-dinner conversations. "However, my father said that if I could convince you that my feelings are sincere, then they would reconsider."

DeWitt rested his arm, the one holding his cup, on the sofa's armrest. "Are you willing to leave your family and your life here and start a new life wherever she is without even knowing if she reciprocates your feelings?"

Despite the man's attempts to make him second-guess his decision, Frank didn't waver. "I've never prayed for more wisdom and direction from God. I've discussed ways and means with my father and grandfather and how I could support a wife. My financials are sound. I am willing to share them if you would like."

"What will you do if I don't give my consent?"

Frank went still. He loved Malia. But he would not ask her to marry him without consent. He would not ask her to dishonor her grandfather like her mother had.

"Sir," he began slowly, "if you refuse, then I will try, through proof of stability, seriousness and good character, to win your approval." He absently picked at a piece of lint on the black trousers of his three-piece suit as he waited for Malia's grandfather to speak.

DeWitt leaned forward, resting his elbows on his knees, his cup on the palm of his hand. He smirked. "And how is that different from what you've been doing these past eight days?"

Frank grinned. "I've never been good with stealth. It's one of my flaws."

"I expect you will need to know where you're headed."

"That would be convenient."

DeWitt stretched out his arm and firmly shook Frank's hand. "Our girl is in Seattle."

*The Bon Marché*
*The corner of Second Avenue and Pike Street*
*Seattle, Washington*
*Independence Day*

"I like your work, Miss Carr." Mrs. Nordhoff wrote something on the notepad on her desk, giving Malia a prime view of the jeweled hair combs given to the widow by her fiancée upon their engagement. "Your window displays were unlike anything we've seen in Seattle. Sales are up in every department."

Malia held her smile as she sat in one of the chairs in front of the department store owner's desk. "Thank you, ma'am."

The woman who couldn't be but a few years older than Malia was nodding. She continued writing.

The rickety bamboo fan overhead added a comfortable breeze to the office. Over breakfast, Malia had read in the Seattle dailies that New York was experiencing a hot spell. The heavy air bearing down on the streets, simmering with heat, proved fatal. In the past week alone, seven hundred people and one thousand horses in the city had died. Thankfully, she had not received any word of personal loss. Still, once work ended for the day, she would place a call to Grandfather, Irene and the Grahames, to see if any had news about Frank, on how he was doing. Wherever that elixir was for curing love's affliction, she had yet to find it.

Malia smoothed the lap of her black skirt.

Mrs. Nordhoff put down her pencil. She glanced up, her gaze seeking Malia's. "Not only did those displays attract shoppers, but I've received calls from The Leader and Frederick & Nelson wanting to know who designed them."

Malia stiffened. Two other department stores wanted to know about her? She swallowed the lump of panic in her throat. "Did you give them my name?"

Mrs. Nordhoff's head tilted as she studied Malia. "That would have benefited neither of us, don't you think?"

Malia released the breath she was holding. She nodded. "I am honored you took a chance and hired me considering my only employment experience is as a governess.

Have you had a chance to review my Christmas display proposal?"

There was a glint in her eyes. "Mr. McDermott and I discussed you with my brother-in-law, Rudolph. We examined your proposal for the Christmas displays and agree it is impressive. We'd like you to begin work on it immediately."

"You would?"

Mrs. Nordhoff's lips twitched with amusement.

"We were so impressed with you volunteering to decorate our window displays for Independence Day, in addition to fulfilling your normal duties, we'd like to promote you to director of displays."

Malia gave her a dubious look. "I didn't know that was a position."

"It wasn't. You showed us we need to have one."

Malia gripped the armrests to keep from jumping to her feet and screaming with joy. Instead, she issued her thanks and walked sedately from Mrs. Nordhoff's office.

Once work was over for the day, she'd hurry home and write Frank a letter. Not that she'd mail it, as she had any of the others. Writing to him every night probably put her in the class of silly Lydia Bennet from *Pride and Prejudice,* but she didn't care. She wanted to follow her heart, and her heart couldn't quite let go of Frank.

The next morning Malia removed the last of the stars-and-stripes fabric from the display wall and laid it in the box with the rest of the decorations. The morning sun streaming through the street-front windows warmed her back. The bells of a trolley clanged as another one turned off Pike and onto Second and passed her window. The trumpeter who played ragtime at the corner hadn't yet arrived. But it wasn't yet noon, his usual time of arrival. She and the hundreds of pedestrians would have the rest of the afternoon to listen to him.

A hand rapped against the glass, but she paid it no mind. With the Bon Marché located in the business heart of the city, window gawkers, usually children and college boys, found it amusing to tap on the window whenever she was working on a display. Ignoring was easier if she wanted to finish her work on time.

Malia stepped back until she was almost at the window. Placing her hands on the hips of her robin's egg blue dress, she took in the emptied space and visualized her sketch coming to life. The beach scene she'd painted on a canvas would fill the back wall nicely. Five mannequins would be too much, though. She needed only an adult one and two children and—

A hand rapped again against the glass with a firmer *rat-a-tat-tat-tat*.

Malia stretched her arm to the side and waved. That usually appeased whoever was watching her. Worse, it could be one of the three deliverymen who had already invited her out for ice after work.

*Rat-a-tat-tat-tat.*

She sighed. She may as well give the attention the person wanted so she could get back to work. Malia turned around. Instead of a person, at eye level was a three-by-four-foot sketch pad with two words in the center—

MALIA CARR

The man, in neatly pressed pin-striped trousers, flipped the page up and over.

Her eyes widened.

WILL YOU MARRY ME?

She laughed. "Is this a joke?" she said, although there was nobody in the store around the display to hear her. Her hand hovered over the glass before she unleashed her own *rat-a-tat-tat-tat*.

The sign lowered.

There, with the cheekiest grin ever, stood Frank.

Her heart found the beat it had been missing since she last saw him. She looked at him askance. "What are you doing here?" she called out and hoped he could hear her through the glass.

He cupped his ear and frowned.

Malia pointed to the Second Avenue entrance. He tucked the sketch pad under his arm and took off jogging. She stepped around boxes and down out of the display window. After allowing two customers to pass, she looked for Frank. He stood several feet away next to a glass jewelry case. He laid his sketch pad on the top.

"I didn't hear your answer." He quirked a smile, the same one she remembered every time she closed her eyes.

Malia walked up to him. "What are you doing here? How did you find me? What are you thinking? Not to mention, why—"

"Whoa there, little lady. I can only handle three questions at a time."

"Little lady?"

"I may have read a few dime novels during the train ride" —his face lost all amusement— "across the *entire* continental United States. You couldn't have chosen Iowa?"

"There's no ocean there," she said with a shrug.

His blue eyes widened. "There's not?"

She chuckled. "Stop avoiding my questions."

He inclined his head to the sketch pad. "That's why I'm here. I found you because I went to the Wizard to ask him for consent to marry his granddaughter." His face screwed up as if he was trying to solve a perplexing puzzle. "I was thinking that I love you."

A squeak came from the jewelry clerk whose hands covered her heart.

Something about his smile made Malia feel as if she were floating out of her skin. A dozen customers were milling about the counters, focusing more on them than the gems in the cabinets, yet she couldn't school her smile or that silly Lydia Bennet giggle. "You were thinking that?"

He looked pained. "I may still be thinking I love you."

"You may?"

"No, I'm pretty sure I do." He stepped closer. "I know it's too soon for us to get married," he said in a serious voice, "but if you give me the benefit of the doubt, over time, you will realize you can trust me, not as a marshal protecting you but as a husband."

Malia stepped closer still. She threaded her fingers through his. "How about we agree to be each other's protector? Each other's best friend."

"Interesting proposal, Miss Carr. I'll watch over you, and you'll watch over me. Hmm." His brow furrowed. "Does that mean I have to keep my eyes on you at all times? Once we're married, of course," he quickly added.

"Oh, well, if that's too much work—"

His finger touched her lips. "Hold that thought." He freed his hand from hers and picked up the sketch pad and gave it to the jewelry clerk. "Would you mind holding it" —he stood it upright— "just like this." The pad blocked them from her view. "Ah, perfect."

Malia pressed her lips together so she wouldn't laugh.

Frank looked at her, cleared his throat, straightened his suit coat and adjusted his tie. "I believe I asked a question you haven't answered."

Her heart clenched. "Yes, I would very much like—"

His hands cradled her face, and his lips found hers, the first touch achingly gentle, a light brush of his lips against hers. Malia gasped. He drew back, questioning her with his eyes. He was gazing at her with such love and restraint. He whispered her name, and she rose to her toes, gripping the front of his jacket with a sense of urgency in her veins. His lips tasted of coffee and crumpets, of wishes fulfilled. Before she knew it, he'd wrapped his arms around her waist, lifting her toes off the ground.

Malia sighed with contentment. Frank may have pursued her, but she found the man she wanted and she wasn't ever going to let go.

Until the floor manager came over and asked what exactly was going on.

To which Frank replied, "Finding home. There's no place like it, you know."

\* \* \* \* \*

# REQUEST YOUR FREE BOOKS!

## 2 FREE INSPIRATIONAL NOVELS
## PLUS 2
# FREE
## MYSTERY GIFTS

*Love Inspired*®

---

**YES!** Please send me 2 FREE Love Inspired® novels and my 2 FREE mystery gifts (gifts are worth about $10). After receiving them, if I don't wish to receive any more books, I can return the shipping statement marked "cancel." If I don't cancel, I will receive 6 brand-new novels every month and be billed just $4.74 per book in the U.S. or $5.24 per book in Canada. That's a savings of at least 21% off the cover price. It's quite a bargain! Shipping and handling is just 50¢ per book in the U.S. and 75¢ per book in Canada.* I understand that accepting the 2 free books and gifts places me under no obligation to buy anything. I can always return a shipment and cancel at any time. Even if I never buy another book, the two free books and gifts are mine to keep forever.

105/305 IDN F49N

| | | |
|---|---|---|
| Name | (PLEASE PRINT) | |
| Address | | Apt. # |
| City | State/Prov. | Zip/Postal Code |

Signature (if under 18, a parent or guardian must sign)

### Mail to the Harlequin® Reader Service:
### IN U.S.A.: P.O. Box 1867, Buffalo, NY 14240-1867
### IN CANADA: P.O. Box 609, Fort Erie, Ontario L2A 5X3

**Are you a subscriber to Love Inspired books
and want to receive the larger-print edition?
Call 1-800-873-8635 or visit www.ReaderService.com.**

* Terms and prices subject to change without notice. Prices do not include applicable taxes. Sales tax applicable in N.Y. Canadian residents will be charged applicable taxes. Offer not valid in Quebec. This offer is limited to one order per household. Not valid for current subscribers to Love Inspired books. All orders subject to credit approval. Credit or debit balances in a customer's account(s) may be offset by any other outstanding balance owed by or to the customer. Please allow 4 to 6 weeks for delivery. Offer available while quantities last.

**Your Privacy**—The Harlequin® Reader Service is committed to protecting your privacy. Our Privacy Policy is available online at www.ReaderService.com or upon request from the Harlequin Reader Service.
We make a portion of our mailing list available to reputable third parties that offer products we believe may interest you. If you prefer that we not exchange your name with third parties, or if you wish to clarify or modify your communication preferences, please visit us at www.ReaderService.com/consumerchoice or write to us at Harlequin Reader Service Preference Service, P.O. Box 9062, Buffalo, NY 14269. Include your complete name and address.

LIDIR13R

# REQUEST YOUR FREE BOOKS!

## 2 FREE INSPIRATIONAL NOVELS
## PLUS 2
# FREE
## MYSTERY GIFTS

*Love Inspired.*
## HISTORICAL
### INSPIRATIONAL HISTORICAL ROMANCE

---

**YES!** Please send me 2 FREE Love Inspired® Historical novels and my 2 FREE mystery gifts (gifts are worth about $10). After receiving them, if I don't wish to receive any more books, I can return the shipping statement marked "cancel." If I don't cancel, I will receive 4 brand-new novels every month and be billed just $4.74 per book in the U.S. or $5.24 per book in Canada. That's a savings of at least 21% off the cover price. It's quite a bargain! Shipping and handling is just 50¢ per book in the U.S. and 75¢ per book in Canada.* I understand that accepting the 2 free books and gifts places me under no obligation to buy anything. I can always return a shipment and cancel at any time. Even if I never buy another book, the two free books and gifts are mine to keep forever.

102/302 IDN F5CY

| | |
|---|---|
| Name | (PLEASE PRINT) |

| | | |
|---|---|---|
| Address | | Apt. # |

| | | |
|---|---|---|
| City | State/Prov. | Zip/Postal Code |

Signature (if under 18, a parent or guardian must sign)

### Mail to the **Harlequin® Reader Service:**
**IN U.S.A.:** P.O. Box 1867, Buffalo, NY 14240-1867
**IN CANADA:** P.O. Box 609, Fort Erie, Ontario L2A 5X3

**Want to try two free books from another series?**
**Call 1-800-873-8635 or visit www.ReaderService.com.**

\* Terms and prices subject to change without notice. Prices do not include applicable taxes. Sales tax applicable in N.Y. Canadian residents will be charged applicable taxes. Offer not valid in Quebec. This offer is limited to one order per household. Not valid for current subscribers to Love Inspired Historical books. All orders subject to credit approval. Credit or debit balances in a customer's account(s) may be offset by any other outstanding balance owed by or to the customer. Please allow 4 to 6 weeks for delivery. Offer available while quantities last.

**Your Privacy**—The Harlequin® Reader Service is committed to protecting your privacy. Our Privacy Policy is available online at www.ReaderService.com or upon request from the Harlequin Reader Service.

We make a portion of our mailing list available to reputable third parties that offer products we believe may interest you. If you prefer that we not exchange your name with third parties, or if you wish to clarify or modify your communication preferences, please visit us at www.ReaderService.com/consumerschoice or write to us at Harlequin Reader Service Preference Service, P.O. Box 9062, Buffalo, NY 14269. Include your complete name and address.

LIHDIR13R

# *Reader Service*.com

## Manage your account online!

- Review your order history
- Manage your payments
- Update your address

---

*We've designed
the Harlequin® Reader Service
website just for you.*

---

## Enjoy all the features!

- Reader excerpts from any series
- Respond to mailings and
  special monthly offers
- Discover new series available to you
- Browse the Bonus Bucks catalog
- Share your feedback

*Visit us at:*

## ReaderService.com

RS13